From C
TO GANJA FIELDS
The Journey Between

Linda Botkin

Outskirts Press, Inc.
Denver, Colorado

From Corn Fields to Ganja Fields
The Journey Between
All Rights Reserved.
Copyright © 2011 Linda Botkin
v2.0

Outskirts Press, Inc.
http://www.outskirtspress.com

ISBN: 978-1-4327-7163-8

Outskirts Press and the "OP" logo are trademarks belonging to Outskirts Press, Inc.

PRINTED IN THE UNITED STATES OF AMERICA

DEDICATION

To Popeye:

For his tireless encouragement to me to write this book and for the
many years he watched my back when things seemed the darkest.

PREFACE

I'm just an ordinary woman who God chose to give an extraordinary life. Why He did I will never know. Maybe if I make it to heaven I can ask Him.

This book is a fictionalized account of actual events. Poetic and literary license have been generously taken in some instances, and in other instances, some details and names have been changed to protect the innocent. But all events are based on information that can be corroborated by documents on record and are as accurate as my memory serves me. I have picked the minds of retired police officers and friends, and along with old, yellowed news clippings and case reports, this book is as close to the truth as possible.

This book is about honest people, and some, not so honest. The ones that inspired me were from both categories and have molded my thinking and the results of this writing. The ones that were dirty politicians and corrupt cops inspired me to expose them. The honest ones are commended for their consistent struggle to walk a straight line in a world that was filled with corruption.

I did not set out to change anything by writing this book. Those years have passed. I gave it much more than the old college try. I endangered my life and that of my family. After retiring, I became a missionary to Jamaica, only to find the drugs and corruption literally at my front door.

Everything I have done, I would do again if I had to. I still have it in me, and the fact is that more than anything in life, I hate injustice. Never should an innocent person be incarcerated, nor should a man who murders be able to walk the streets free. But in Delaware County,

Muncie, Indiana, as well as Jamaica, that's how it goes. The good ole' boys who drink together, break the law together, turn their heads, and have made a pact. Theirs was a strong pact indeed. They stick together no matter what—lawyers, judges, prosecutors, deputy prosecutors, deputy sheriffs, police officers, and prosecutors' investigators. This is why Muncie, Indiana, is known as "Little Chicago," and Jamaica is called the murder capital of the world.

Until the "big boys" roll up their sleeves and clean up the mess, it will go on forever. I hope I live that long to see that happen, but I'm not holding my breath.

INTRODUCTION

Kit had always had an exciting life. As a high school student she had promised herself that she would never be bored. She had always wanted to live on the edge, and one thing for sure—that she did. Some would even say a little too close to the edge sometimes. But all that had changed. Through her efforts and with the help of a tight-knit group of trusted and dedicated officers, a corrupt FBI agent was ordered to "retire" following an investigation and sting operation, and word was already on the street that the new "bosses" were definitely out to get her for initiating the massive investigation of the courthouse crew. There was also the matter of the many police officers still in her own squad who were tied to the prosecutor; a dangerous situation for Kit as there were not many officers she could trust.

In the early '70s, marijuana (ganja) was flooding the United States. While it had always been widely used in other states—New York, New Jersey, Florida, and California, chief among them, it was relatively new to the Midwest. And in Muncie, Indiana, it was getting worse with each passing day.

At first, the drug runners in Indiana didn't seem to be so evident and out there in your face. They operated in the shadows and were controlled and protected by prosecutors, judges, sheriffs, and police chiefs. It was a very hard line to prove that corrupt officials were raking in loads of money from the trafficking of the weed. But Kit had beaten the bushes for years to track the money and connect them to the thriving ganja distribution enterprises of the Florida importers, then on to the source where it was grown.

The job of policing got more dangerous, and no matter how many hours were put in by undercover cops, the beat went on. It had become epidemic in nature, the streets full of drug dealers, and, of course, thieves and an upsurge of prostitution to feed habits. This was a concern to the general public in Muncie, especially parents whose kids were getting involved and who saw their sons and daughters turning into crackheads.

So much money was pouring in from the lucrative cocaine and marijuana trade that dealers had to find creative ways to launder the money. There seemed to be an upsurge of new "businesses" being registered on a daily basis. Certain lawyers in the town seemed to have struck the mother lode. It was on these lawyers that Kit had focused her attention.

As chief of investigations, Kit had sent her men from the Intelligence Division to collect the trash each morning from the courthouse and a certain lawyer's office that the division had under surveillance. It was alarming to see how many "businesses" were being registered by the lawyer and a check on the addresses of the "new businesses" showed that they were located in vacant houses in run-down areas of the city.

Anyone with any brains at all could figure out what was happening. The businesses were set up to run the dirty money through. But the team's luck ran out when the lawyer got wind of the officers' daily pickup and started doing something else with their trash. Kit suspected that her team had been "ratted out" by a police captain and was convinced that her division had been doubled-crossed by the FBI. It was obvious that policemen were being bribed, and it became patently clear to all when a patrolman who made $20,000 a year bought a brand-new Cadillac for cash.

In response, Kit drew her little band of loyal and honest cops tighter for security reasons, not trusting anyone outside of the group. It was common knowledge that the FBI agent was a drunkard who talked freely when he drank with the courthouse crew and the same FBI agent was in charge of the district. It was also becoming clear that all the information given to the FBI agent was being discussed over drinks in a bar. How else could sensitive information that had been given only to the FBI become common knowledge?

Kit and her investigating team knew that too many leaks could result in the investigation being compromised, or worse. And the truth is they were a small band of officers who were fighting a giant problem with the cards stacked against them. But they were determined to carry on fighting the drug cartel and the good ole' boys club that couldn't keep their mouths shut when they drank together each week.

Through the hard work and diligence of her team, Kit succeeded in making a solid and convincing case, and the corrupt FBI agent was ordered to "retire" following an investigation and sting operation that had reached all the way to the prosecutor's office and the courthouse itself.

For her efforts, she had been shot at and threatened, her men had been shot at, and the safety of her family had been challenged. And to further emphasize the point that no good deed goes unpunished, the prosecutor's office had filed a multimillion-dollar lawsuit against her in an effort to intimidate her and have her back off the case.

A family vacation or cruise would be a wonderful way to relax and make the family connection. Kit had always been in love with the sea. The idea of sunshine and beaches with white, powdery sand gave her joy just imagining them, so when she saw the brochures in the local travel agency, she did not hesitate to book a cruise for the family. It was a seven-day cruise in the Caribbean. She had never been out of the USA so it was exciting to think of cruising to Mexico, the Cayman Islands, Jamaica, and the Bahamas. This would also be the ideal time to bond with her husband Mel, a retired schoolteacher.

It seemed that she and Mel had been going in different directions. Mel was an A-type personality, on the move all the time and really never seeing marriage as a priority. He was a workaholic whose focus was on whatever made him the most money at the time. He was never abusive, for which Kit was thankful, but her needs were always on the back burner. He was selfish, into himself, prideful, boastful, and put himself first in every situation. A very hard to love person, but she gave it her best try.

Life with Mel continued in what she described as "a give-give marriage." She did the all giving, but chose to roll with it after she learned that her input never really mattered a hoot to him anyway. She had continued on with her life as best she could, and thankfully, Mel never objected much to what she did, as long as it didn't interfere with his plans. Looking back, she was amazed that they made it through all their years of marriage. There was never a real connection with him, never a "real love" connection, just husband and wife living as strangers most of the time. Kit looked forward to some time to try to rekindle the fires and reconnect with Mel.

CHAPTER ONE

IN THE BEGINNING

It was delightful as we pulled into the Caribbean ports. But it was Jamaica that took my breath away. We had spent the night anchored offshore, just outside the island's territorial waters. The twinkling lights on land were barely visible, and, in the complete blackness of the tropical night, could easily be mistaken for stars. The plan was for the ship to arrive in the Montego Bay port in the morning.

As the ship pulled into the harbor, the passengers were all crowded on the viewing decks, getting our first look of the island. I could not believe my eyes. It was awesomely beautiful. The sparkling beauty of the sea, with lush green mountains rising up in the background, shrouded in clouds and mist, provided stark contrast with the bustling port with its fleet of tour buses and taxis lined up, waiting to transport the ship's passengers on various tours of the island. Our tour was of the southwestern coast of the island and according to the brochure, would "culminate in lunch at a Great House in the hills of Westmoreland." The girls wanted to say on board and not do the day trip.

The lilting, musical sound of the local dialect as the drivers and immigration and customs officials addressed each other was music to my ears. It reminded me of the sing-song sound of the Irish kids I had known growing up in Indiana and brought a smile to my face.

Maybe it was the warm trade winds blowing, embracing me as it blew by, or maybe it was God whispering in my ear; but whatever it was as we disembarked the ship and boarded the bus assigned to our group, I could not contain my excitement. I knew in my heart and soul that I would return to this beautiful island. *It was like a whispering in my ear, an almost audible voice telling me I would be returning to this island.*

Wait, I said to myself, *I have not even put my foot down on the solid ground, so why am I feeling this way?*

"Wouldn't it be great if we could live here?" I gushed to Mel. I guess he didn't share my excitement, because he just grunted his usual, "Huh?"

I was not ready to give up, so I gave it the old Midwestern try after we settled in our seats in the bus and the driver pulled out of the port. We were headed along the road that would take us round the western part of the island to the parish of Westmoreland.

"Come on, think about it, honey: warm sunshine all year-round; no snow to shovel; no wood to chop; swimming in the ocean. Come on, Mel, who wouldn't love that?" But he just stared at me, so I decided to give it a rest and enjoy the passing scenery.

The drive along the coast was scary but exciting. The roads seemed very narrow to me, but then again, I was used to the highways of America. But not only were they narrow and winding, but also pock-marked with many potholes and in some instances, craters. I was amazed and impressed with the way the bus driver navigated the road with great skill and ease. In an attempt to ease the tension with Mel, I tried to make light of the drive. "Wow, this guy is good, Mel. He could certainly run rings around the guys at the motocross track when it comes to dexterity," I joked.

Mel was not impressed with me making light of his venture. "Maybe you think he can run rings around those guys, but just because you think a thing is so, that doesn't make it so." His voice dripped with sarcasm and barely restrained anger. Seemed I had touched a nerve.

My husband, whose middle name is work, a few years before, had talked me into buying a forty-five-acre farm with a dog kennel and a motocross track. He really had no interest in the kennel and animals and only wanted the race track. It was really what he wanted so I had taken some of my savings out of the bank and put the down payment on it. Mel was supposed to make the payments after that from the proceeds of the race track. His drivers were more used to driving tractors than cars, however, and had had quite a few mishaps.

As we drove along the coast, I stared out the bus window and the thoughts came unbidden as I couldn't help but reflect on my life and ponder the future. So far, the attempt to bring back the fire in the marriage had failed. Mel just didn't show any interest in my attempts to be relaxed and romantic. He was silent and sullen or sarcastic and whining. Seven days at sea was too much for him. The rest and relaxation was "boring." He needed to have constant activity. I was at a loss. I had always put my feelings on the back burner with him and kept on keeping on. I wanted my marriage to Mel to work.

My first marriage at age twenty had crumbled after four years and one child. My first husband Dan had been violent with a temper that was always on edge. He hit me many times, but I had been young and foolish when I got involved with him.

CHAPTER TWO

YOUNG LOVE

I was a virgin when I met Dan, and we dated for two years. On our wedding night, after a brief ceremony at city hall and a hamburger at the Pixie Din ,er checked into the sleazy motel that we really couldn't afford, but I had insisted on for a honeymoon. I even had a lacy night-gown I had bought from a thrift store for a dollar.

We started our married life living in Florida in a one-room apart-ment that we paid forty dollars a month for. The apartment, while small with peeling paint on the walls, was our first home, and I set about making it as cozy as possible. I convinced Dan to buy an old, beat-up, plaid couch from the same thrift store where I bought my honeymoon nightie. The sofa opened out at night into a bed, and when you opened the fridge door, you hit the stove. But it was home.

Dan was a hairstylist and brought home a guaranteed salary of eighteen dollars per week. In Florida at that time, the minimum wage was one dollar an hour, and jobs were hard to find, so we were there-fore grateful for the small salary. After paying rent, utilities, and the note on a broken-down car that Dan insisted he needed, there was maybe five dollars left for food.

Three months after our wedding, I discovered I was pregnant. When I delivered the news, it was not welcomed by Dan. "How could you do this to me?" he screamed when I gave him the news. "We barely have enough money to feed us now. How are we going to feed a baby too?"

I was dumbfounded. "How could *I* do this to you? What did I do except what you wanted me to do?" I yelled before I had time to think. "How selfish can you be? This is *our* child we are discussing. I thought

∽ 4 ∾

…" But I did not have time to finish my sentence. The slap across my face laid me out flat on the ground, left me with a ringing in my ears for two days, and it took a week for the swelling and black and blue to fade.

As I lay on the ground sobbing and holding my jaw, Dan seemed to snap out of a trance and realize what he had done. He immediately gathered me into his arms, rocking me like a baby, tears streaming down his face. "See what you caused? See what you made me do? Please forgive me, Kit. I didn't mean to lash out at you, but you have to understand, I have a bad temper."

It was pathetic to watch him beg and plead for forgiveness. It was never in my nature to hold a grudge, and this was my new husband, so I cradled his face in my hands, kissed him, and told him I loved him and forgave him. And so began a routine that would define the pattern of our life together. He would beat me, and then would feel so sorry and miserable, and I would feel so sorry for him that my heart would melt and I could not remain angry. And so the cycle began and continued.

CHAPTER THREE

ORANGE GROVES

From the very beginning, my pregnancy did not go well. I was malnourished, dehydrated, and weak. And Dan was often missing in action. During the day he was at work at the salon where he did women's hair, and after work he was out "with the boys" every night. The money he used to provide for food became less and less, and sometimes not at all. To keep the hunger away, I ate the odd candy bar and the rotten oranges that I managed to salvage from a Dumpster outside the orange grove's fence.

Our apartment was in a run-down complex on the edge of an orange grove. Really, the complex was little more than a flophouse for the migrant workers that worked in the groves, picking and packing the fruit. All those lovely oranges you see in mesh bags in the supermarkets and airport shops came from these groves. The grove was surrounded by chain-link fences on all sides. The fence rose about seven feet into the air and was topped with three strands of razor-sharp barbed wire. I discovered a place in the fence where I could climb over so on days when I felt brave, I would climb through and fetch fresh oranges. A big sign loomed over me stating that a jail term of six months and a $500 fine awaited anyone caught stealing oranges, but I didn't care ... I was hungry.

When we first moved to the apartment, I had asked the security guard at the gate if I could apply for a job inside. The amused look on his face as he eyed me up and down belied the sharp tone of his voice. "This is no work for you, sweet thing. You are a nice, white lady. This work is for the wetbacks, Cubans, and Jamaicans. They can manage the hot sun. They are born to it." I didn't say it, but I would have gladly become a "wetback," whatever that was, and I longed to be Cuban or Jamaican.

By the time I was six months pregnant, our lives had deteriorated to beyond desperate, and one evening, after I had spent the day drinking water from the tap and sucking on ketchup packages from the local restaurant in town, I got up the courage to confront Dan, hoping that I might be able to get him to take an interest in the baby.

"Rotten oranges, candy bars, and the odd hunk of bread with ketchup is not the kind of diet that anybody should live on, much less a pregnant mother," I yelled, as he tried his best to ignore me. But, maybe it was hunger, or maybe it was just that I was tired of being tired, but I just wouldn't let it go. I tried to sound more reasonable. "You need to take more interest in our baby. You need to be more responsible, Dan," I pleaded. "You're going to be a father soon. You need to start staying home some more, Dan."

The reaction was immediate and swift. The blow to the side of my head rocked my head back and forth, while white lights and black spots exploded in my eyes. I fell to the ground, splayed like a Raggedy Ann doll, looking up at my enraged husband.

"I have no interest in being a father," he yelled, his fists bunched at his side. "I'm not ready to be tied down by a brat. You need to get that in your head," he informed me as I struggled to get up, and he shoved me back to the floor with his foot. As my head slammed into the floor, he put his foot on my throat and applied enough pressure so that I passed out. I don't know how long I was out for, but when I came to, he was gone.

When he returned home two days later, he was dirty, his pants looked as if he had wet himself, his face was shadowed by a scruffy two-day beard and his red-rimmed eyes were set in dark, sunken sockets. He smelled as if he had bathed in skunk juice and cheap corn liquor. And he was carrying a big paper-wrapped gift box and a bouquet of flowers. As soon as he walked through the door, we both burst out crying.

His apology was tearful and penitent. "Baby girl, I am so sorry," he wailed, smoothing back the hair from my forehead. "You know I love you, don't you? I just can't help myself," he sobbed. The tears worked their magic on me. My heart melted immediately.

"That's okay, honey. I know that you love me. And I'm sorry for getting you angry. It was my fault for getting on you." And so another dimension was added to the pattern. It was always my fault when he abused me.

The flowers were wild flowers he had picked from a field near the orange grove. The paper-wrapped box contained a baby blanket, a towel, and a Onesies. It was the only time that Dan ever gave me a present, and the only things he ever bought for our child.

CHAPTER FOUR

DAN'S BOYS

After that, I stayed out of his way as much as possible to make sure that Dan didn't pay much attention to me. He did not notice that I looked like a scarecrow that had swallowed a basketball. I was all skin and bones, with skin that hung off my lanky five foot eight inch frame like an old woman's, and my small belly was the size of an underinflated basketball. In fact, I was alone most of the time. Dan was hardly ever around now, except when he needed to change clothes or grab a quick shower or crash for a few hours. Some nights he did not come home at all. And most times, when he did come home, he would often come home high on alcohol and accompanied by one of his "boys."

Dan's "boys" were Chaz, Barry, and JoJo, three guys he met in a local bar. They had become inseparable, cruising in Dan's beat-up old car, hanging out at the pool hall on the outskirts of town every night, hustling migrant workers at pool, and drinking cheap beer. The "boys" did not have jobs but still managed to have enough money to dress in new clothes every day. Chaz, who was blond and cute, had a fondness for expensive leather jeans that looked two sizes too small for his muscled legs and butt, lizard and snakeskin cowboy boots, and tight black T-shirts with the sleeves rolled up over his pack of cigarettes. I used to wonder if he wasn't burning up, wearing leather pants in the muggy Florida heat.

Barry, a transplant from New York, was a little more conservative, favoring khakis, bright Hawaiian shirts under linen jackets, and hand-made Italian penny loafers. The leather was always clean and buffed, and the pennies in the slot in the front of the shoes were always shiny. There were times when I was so hungry, I thought of asking him for them. I could at least buy a candy bar with them. But Dan wouldn't have liked that, and in any event, he didn't allow me to speak with any of the boys.

JoJo, a farm boy from Tennessee, wore sleeveless, plaid work shirts tucked into blue denim Levis that fitted like a second skin. He always had a bandana handkerchief tied around his head, topped by a leather cowboy hat. Another bandana, neatly folded, hung from the back pocket of his jeans. The cuffs of the jeans were rolled over motorcycle boots that were embellished with silver chains, buckles, and studs.

They were quite a contrast to Dan. When I first met him, I thought Dan was the most gorgeous guy I had ever laid eyes on. He carried his six foot frame with confidence and moved with a catlike grace. His chiseled features and dimpled chin gave him the rugged look of a handsome movie star—a cross between James Dean and Kirk Douglas. The first time he spoke with me, I couldn't believe that such a handsome guy was interested in me.

Because of his job at the hair salon and aided by his lack of ready cash, Dan wasn't able to dress in flamboyant or expensive clothes. His only deviation from the pair of black chinos and short-sleeve, button-down shirt he was required to wear at the salon was the black leather vest he would put over the shirt when he went out with the boys. He also decided to grow his hair out and wore it curly and long down to his collar, which was very unusual for a man in Florida in nineteen sixty.

I must confess that I much preferred him with his long hair hanging loose. When he went out at night with the boys, he would wear his hair slicked back in a ponytail, also unusual for the time. The slicked-back hair pulled tight by a black leather thong made his face almost too pretty, but with a sinister cast.

CHAPTER FIVE

MISSING IN ACTION

The day our daughter was born, Dan was nowhere around. He had been missing in action with the boys for about a week. I really was not sure how long he had been gone. When the little food I had at home ran out and the hunger pains gripped my protesting stomach, the days sort of ran into each other for me, and sometimes it was hard to judge how much real time had passed.

As I entered the final stages of my pregnancy and my due date got closer, the lack of proper nutrition had begun to take its toll on me. I became very ill and could barely speak. I was so weak that when I tried to speak, only a whisper came out. I spent most of my time in bed, so weakened by lack of food I could barely lift my head from the pillow.

When the contractions started, I knew it was more than hunger pains. The suddenness and sharpness of the pain was different. It felt as if I had been punched in the stomach with a metal fist. It was worse than all the bad pains I had ever experienced, put together. It was ten times worse than that. As I doubled over in pain on the couch I felt a wetness between my thighs and looked down. The tattered cotton housedress that I was wearing was soaked with blood. Of course, I panicked immediately. "It's not supposed to be blood. It should be water," my mind screamed. "It should be water!!"

I remembered very clearly, at the beginning when I found out I was pregnant, I had scrimped and saved my pennies until I managed to save ten cents. I had exchanged the pennies with one of the women who picked oranges at the orange grove and who lived in the apartment complex for the dime it took to make a telephone call. I had stood in line, waited my turn, and had called my mother from the pay phone the migrant workers used to call home. When I told her I was expecting a baby, I had asked her how I would know when the baby was coming. I remember she had very clearly said, "When your water breaks and the pain starts cutting through you like a hot knife in butter, you will know that the baby is coming." The pain was there all right, but there was no water, just dark red blood. Something was very wrong.

It was certain that my baby and I would die if we did not get help, and that gave my legs the strength to propel me off the couch. I was very weak and dehydrated and barely made it to the door of our apartment and opened the door when the next wave of pain came crashing down on me. The scream that erupted out of me was heard at the other end of the apartment complex and brought the few migrant workers who were home running to see who was dying. Luckily, one of the men who came out to look had an old battered car. He offered to drive me to the local hospital. Two other men had to help lift me to the car.

When we reached the hospital, I was admitted immediately. The sight of my tattered dress which was completely soaked with blood made the emergency room team immediately call for blood for an emergency transfusion. As I lay on the stretcher in the examining room in the emergency room area, the one thought running through my mind was *Dan, where are you?*

But those thoughts were immediately interrupted by the pain that knifed through my body as if a hot poker had been shoved through my guts and what looked to me like all the blood in my body seemed to flow out of me. I passed out as they wheeled me from the emergency room, the lights overhead flashing as the stretcher rolled along a long green corridor. The last thing I remembered before the lights went out was a doctor calling a code blue.

CHAPTER SIX

NEW PROBLEMS

I didn't know how long I was unconscious, but when I woke up, I realized that I was in a room, in a bed, with needles stuck in my arms and tubes running from the needles to a bag of blood and a bag of clear liquid hanging on a metal pole. I was groggy and unable to move or focus my thoughts well, but I fought against the unconsciousness that threatened to swallow me again.

As my eyes adjusted to the dark around me and my mind cleared little by little, things began to come back to me. I immediately looked down to my stomach and saw that the underinflated basketball was gone. The panic welled up in me as the words formed in my mind and worked their way to my lips. *"My baby!"* I thought I shouted, but it only came out like a croak, as the darkness swallowed me again.

When I came awake the second time, a doctor and nurse were standing at the foot of the bed. The doctor, who had been making a notation on a chart on a clipboard, noticed me stirring and looked up from his writing.

"Well, well. Sleeping Beauty is awake," he joked in that hearty voice doctors all seem to have. I was in no mood for jokes.

"My baby?" I croaked, struggling to raise myself up from the bed. The doctor and nurse both rushed to the sides of my bed, arms outstretched, to stop me. They needn't have bothered.

I was still so weak I dropped back onto the pillow.

"Careful, my dear, you still have a ways to go before you will be strong enough to get up," the nurse said sternly. Her voice, while not harsh, did not have the heartiness of the doctor's. She was more matter-of-fact like a caring but stern mother.

The doctor rested his chart on the bed and took my wrist in his hand, checking my pulse with his finger. "You gave us quite a scare there for a moment, Sleeping Beauty," he said again.

"Please, you must tell me what has happened to my baby," I pleaded, my eyes searching his face as if the answer were written on it.

"Your baby is in the nursery," he said reassuringly, still holding on to my hand. "She had to be put in an incubator, but she will be all right."

"I have a daughter?" I burst out, a shadow of a smile on my face. "Oh, thank you, Lord," I breathed as a sigh of relief escaped me. But then that relief was short-lived. "What's wrong with her? What's an incubator?" I asked, my voice stronger but full of anxiety.

"It's nothing for you to worry about. It's like a warm, closed crib and is just a precaution," he explained. "It keeps the baby safe and allows us to monitor her vital signs and give her oxygen if she needs it. You don't have to worry. Once you are strong enough, Nurse Jennings here will take you to the nursery so you can see her," he assured me. "But there is something," he said, his voice turning serious again. "I can't keep calling you Sleeping Beauty. Who are you, my dear? What is your name?"

That's when I realized that nobody at the hospital knew who I was. The migrant workers who brought me to the hospital had left after they took me to the emergency room. Most migrant workers were usually illegal immigrants from countries where mistrust of authorities was the key to self-preservation. They had taken a risk to bring me to the hospital, but didn't stick around to be asked questions.

"My name is Kit Jameson, I mean, Mrs. Katherine Millman, but everybody calls me Kit," I stammered, looking a little embarrassed. Since I had married Dan, nobody had ever asked me my name. I didn't meet that many people, only Dan's boys and the migrant workers at the apartment building. And to them, I was plain "Kit."

"And where is Mr. Millman, Katherine? Can we contact him for you?" Nurse Jennings asked in her stern, motherly voice.

There it was: The question I dreaded answering, since I really didn't have an answer. "I … He … He's … I …" I stammered as the tears welled up in my eyes. "I don't know where he is," I finally managed to choke out. "He went to work last week, and he hasn't come home yet," I explained.

Maybe it was the look in my eyes, or maybe it was just that he was a kind man, but the doctor motioned to the nurse with his head, and she followed him to the door of the room where they had a brief, whispered conversation before returning to my bedside.

"Okay, Katherine," he said, holding out his hand for a handshake, "pleased to meet you. I am Dr. Johnson. Nurse Jennings's name you already know." I knew he was being nice and polite to make me feel better, so I tried to put a good face on.

"Don't worry, Dr. Johnson, when he gets home the neighbors will tell him I am at the hospital, and he will come to take us home," I said, hoping that it was true and that Dan would come soon to the hospital for us.

CHAPTER SEVEN

QUESTIONS

Dr. Johnson and Nurse Jennings did not leave my room, and instead of the kind voice he had used before, Dr. Johnson's tone was hard and even more serious than Nurse Jennings's. "Well, we need to talk with your husband, Katherine. We need to ask him some questions. Questions like why you were half-starved, why you were so dehydrated and malnourished that your amniotic fluid had dried up. Why he has endangered you and your baby. Why you were left alone when you were so close to your delivery." Even though his voice was stern, his face still had a kindly look.

Hot tears flooded my eyes and rolled down my cheeks. I could not look at either the doctor or the nurse as shame coursed through my entire being. But, as usual, I rushed to take the blame. "He couldn't help it, Doctor. It's my fault. He has to go away to work to support us," I lied. "He can't help it," I repeated. The look that passed between Dr. Johnson and Nurse Jennings clearly indicated that they did not buy my explanations, but would leave it alone for now.

Doctor Johnson's voice took on his hearty bedside manner tone again as he picked up my chart from the bed where he had rested it and made another note. "Well, we have to focus on getting you better. We are going to continue the drip—it has medicine as well as vitamins and nutrients in it, and you need it to rehydrate and nourish your body. You need a lot of rest," he explained, as Nurse Jennings folded her arms across her breasts, clearly displeased with him not pursuing the matter of Dan further.

"Hopefully, you will be able to start taking liquids and nourishment by mouth in the next day or two, but for now, we will keep the drip. As soon as you are stronger, you can go see the baby. Rest now, so that you can regain your strength."

It took four more days before I was taken off the drip, and as soon as the drip was disconnected, Nurse Jennings wheeled me in a wheelchair to the nursery to see my baby for the first time. As I saw the tiny pink body squirming and kicking in the incubator, I uttered a silent prayer thanking God for having brought us through our ordeal. "Can I touch her?" I asked Nurse Jennings hopefully.

But she shook her head. "It's still too soon," she said sadly. I could only look at my baby through the glass of the incubator.

My daughter's face was wrinkled like a dried prune, and like all newborns, with her round, bald head, she looked like that old Englishman, Winston Churchill, but without the big cigar. As I gazed at that wrinkled face, it was the most beautiful face I had ever laid eyes on, and my heart swelled with so much love I felt it would burst. And once again, I was shedding tears that scalded my cheeks and dropped into my hands that I did not realize were clasped in my lap as if I were holding my baby.

Nurse Jennings took a tissue from her uniform pocket and handed it to me. She had thawed a little over the days, but still maintained her serious demeanor. "Hush now," she cooed. "She's going to be fine. It will take a little time for her to develop, but she'll be fine. You'll see," she said, trying to sound reassuring.

As she wheeled me back to my room, she tried to ease my sadness at leaving the nursery. "So, what have you decided to name her?" she asked brightly. And for the first time, I realized that I did not have a clue what I would name my daughter.

I had never thought about it before, and Dan was so uninvolved in my pregnancy, we had never discussed names. But I couldn't tell Nurse Jennings that, so I blurted out the first name that came to mind: "Lynette," I said brightly as if I had planned it all along.

"Is that a family name?" Nurse Jennings inquired.

"Yes," I lied, while silently asking God's forgiveness for the untruth. "It was Dan's grandmother's name," I added, compounding the lie. "We decided to call the baby Lynette if it was a girl and Lyndon if it was a boy." I was saved from any further lies, since we had reached my room.

I remained in the hospital for another week before the baby was out of the incubator and the doctor pronounced me well enough to go home. But in all that time, Dan still did not show up, and now that I was ready to go home, I realized that I had no clothes to wear and nothing for the baby to wear home. When I had been rushed to the hospital, nobody had thought to bring the blanket and the onesies Dan had bought for the baby.

It was Nurse Jennings who provided the solution to my dilemma. When Dan had not shown up at the hospital after I had been there for three days, Nurse Jennings had discussed my situation with the pastor of her church. She really did not believe me that my husband was away working. In fact, she really did not believe that I had a husband.

The church which she attended was nondenominational and had a community outreach program to provide assistance to unwed mothers and children who were at risk. In Nurse Jennings's eyes, Lynette and I qualified on both counts. So she had asked the pastor to consider enrolling us in the church's program.

The day I was scheduled to leave the hospital, the pastor, accompanied by Nurse Jennings, presented me with a bag that had three new dresses, a pair of shoes, underwear, and a nightgown. This was accompanied by a basket filled with canned vegetables and canned soups, flour, milk, cheese, crackers, and a loaf of bread. There was also a baby bag with cloth diapers, little frilly dresses, booties and socks, baby oil, baby powder, powdered formula, baby bottles, safety pins; all the things a baby needed. Inside the outside pocket of the bag was an envelope with twenty dollars, which was the most money I had held in my hand since I had married Dan.

And as if that weren't enough, the pastor offered to drive me home. As he did this, he told me that he had arranged with the owner of the local pizza parlor for him to hire me as a counter clerk as soon as I was well enough to work. I wouldn't have to worry about Lynette, since the church ran a crèche in their basement as part of their community outreach program, and I would be able to leave her there during the day while I was at work. Again, the tears came flowing down my cheeks. I seemed to be crying a lot recently, but these tears were tears of joy and gratitude.

The generosity and kindness of the pastor and Nurse Jennings were overwhelming. They made a profound impression on me that people who didn't know me from a hole in the wall cared enough to bring us food, clothes, and money. I made a vow at that point to try to emulate their generosity and kindness, no matter what it took.

CHAPTER EIGHT
TRAPPED

W hen the pastor dropped me off outside our apartment complex, I was happy at my new prospects, but terrified about
what I would face with Dan. What on earth was going to happen to us
and our new baby? I was trapped in hell, with no way to get out. I had
been so green and stupid to think that life would be fantastic with Mr.
Wonderful and feeling loved for the first time in my life. I was stupid
to believe it would be a life of happy ever after. I had given my heart to
a man that I now realized was a monster.

As I walked through our apartment door, cradling my daughter in
my arms, I vowed that I would make sure that she would never make
the same mistakes I had made. And it was a promise I intended to keep.

Dan came home late that night. When he walked through the door,
looking and smelling like he needed a shower, he seemed surprised
to see me holding Lynette in my arms in our bed. I was feeding her
formula in a bottle from the supplies in the care package the pastor
had given me. My breast milk had dried up before the baby was born
because of dehydration.

Maybe it was the rest and nutrition I had gotten in the hospital;
maybe it was the fact that when I looked in my daughter's face as I fed
her from a bottle, I saw a look of pure love and trust; maybe it was that
I was tired of the abusive behavior, but I was determined to hold Dan
accountable. "You need to go take a shower before you come near this
bed," I said to him. "This is my two-week-old daughter Lynette. She
just spent two weeks in an incubator in the hospital, and she doesn't
need to catch anything from you."

The cold tone of my voice and the shards of ice that was my stare made an impact on Dan. I had never had the nerve to stand up to him before, and he was used to having me weak and cowering. He had never seen me in any way other than docile and compliant. He took me seriously and without a word, headed straight to the bathroom. When he emerged half an hour later, he was washed, scrubbed, and clean shaven, and his hair was slicked back with water. He looked liked a penitent schoolboy, begging forgiveness from his mother for some childish prank.

I was not biting the bait this time. I would not fall for the usual tricks. I was determined to protect my daughter. "We have to talk, Dan. We have a lot to talk about," I said in that same cold voice, but without the look, since I was smiling in my daughter's beautiful, sleeping face.

Dan realized that I was not going to give in to his manipulation and sat quietly at the edge of the bed. I know he expected me to cry and shout and berate him, but I really had no interest in that kind of behavior.

"I really do not want to know where you have been in the weeks before I went to the hospital; I don't want to know where you have been for the two weeks after I had gone to the hospital; I don't even want to know why you didn't come to the hospital to look for us. In fact, I don't even need to know why you prefer to spend your time with strange men, rather than with your wife. I don't need to know any of that.

"What I need to know is how you intend to take care of and provide for our daughter who is, thank God, sleeping soundly, in clothes given to her by total strangers, on a foldout couch."

CHAPTER NINE
MOVE TO MUNCIE

By the end of the month, we returned to Muncie and moved into the four-room, upstairs apartment in my parents' home. Had we stayed in Florida any longer, I'm not sure what would have happened. We shared a bathroom that had mushrooms growing in the damp shower stall, but at least we didn't have to pay rent. I was also not so isolated anymore. I had my parents nearby and was back home in my own environment.

Dan got another job in a beauty shop. He had bleached his hair blond and was now calling himself "Mr. Dan." He still was not making much money, and even with not paying rent, we still could not keep up with day-to-day living and the needs of a new baby. Babies are expensive. If every teenager who has ever contemplated unprotected sex knew ahead of time the real, financial, physical, and emotional cost of a baby, there would be a significant decrease in teen pregnancies.

After a couple months of Dan sweating to buy formula, diapers, and all the must-haves for a baby, I talked him into letting me get a job. The Pizza Parlor across the alley from my parents' home had an opening for a counter clerk. It seemed to me to me that God was pointing me toward work in the world of pizza. I didn't get the opportunity to take up the offer of the job in the pizza parlor in Florida, but God had provided the chance again.

CHAPTER TEN

GOOD COPS, BAD COPS

I worked nights, and Dan worked days. This enabled one of us to always watch our baby girl. Dan would come home from the beauty parlor by 5:00 p.m. so that I could duck across the alley from our house and slip into the back door of the parlor, and still claim the full shift hours of the five-midnight shift.

While leaving my baby every evening was difficult and painful in the beginning, I soon overcame those feelings and settled into making the best of the job. The guaranteed paycheck, a quarter above the minimum wage of one dollar an hour, though small, made a huge difference to our lives. Combined with the cash tips I received, my salary was almost as much as Dan's. He had now moved up to two dollars an hour, plus tips. My salary was providing us with a measure of financial stability that we had never enjoyed before.

I was also enjoying the interaction with the people who came into the pizza parlor. They were a varied and different bunch. Nighttime in a pizza joint in Midwest USA is the same all over. The characters and personalities would provide a complete library of psychological and psychiatric terms, but to me, they were just everyday people.

There were the regulars—the cocky teenagers who swaggered in as if they owned the place, but who were really just wannabe hoods and aspiring criminals; the poor single mother who comes in every evening after she had finished a day washing dishes in a restaurant downtown near the courthouse. She sits wearily at the same corner booth with her back to the wall but a good view of the door, and shares her order, a single slice of cheese pizza, sliced three ways, and a large soda with two straws, with her two toddlers. This is dinner for them.

Then there was the everyday working Joe who stops in to grab a slice to go while he is on the way to the night shift; and finally, there were the cops.

Most of all I was fascinated by the cops. I had not given up on my dream as a high school teenager to one day follow my brother and become a law enforcement officer, and I still remembered the old chief's promise that he would give me a job when I was twenty-one years old if I was still interested and could pass the requisite training and exams.

There were good cops and bad cops. There were cops that came regularly to the parlor to get a bite to eat or just to sit for a while and take a break from pounding the beat. There were cops who huddled with strange-looking characters in the dark corner near the bathroom, and there were the cops who seemed to just loiter from time to time, watching the world go by. This was my first look at the world in which the men in blue live.

The pizza parlor owner had made it his policy, "as part of his civic duty," as he termed it, to never charge a cop for his pizza. So the cops all came in to take advantage of his largesse, and it ensured a measure of security that few other businesses enjoyed. The owner was often heard bragging that "the pizza parlor operates without fear of being robbed or vandalized. We have the best security!"

CHAPTER ELEVEN
UNDERCURRENT

Dan also seemed to have settled into the routine our lives had taken, but I had an uneasy sense of a seething undercurrent. As the months passed, I was beginning to see a lot of anger in Dan. While he didn't seem to mind watching Lynette while I was at work, on the odd occasion when I would get a night off, he opted to go out "for some air and some male company," rather than spend time with the two of us. It was apparent to me that since we had returned to Indiana, he had grown even more distant than he was in Florida.

It was with this in mind that one night, when Lynette was just past her first birthday and I had the night off, I decided to surprise Dan with a romantic dinner. I did not tell him that I had the evening off, and spent the afternoon exhausting my culinary repertoire of chicken smothered in gravy, mashed potatoes, and green beans. I had snagged a burnt down candle and empty wine bottle from the pizza parlor and placed it in the center of the table. It wasn't much, but it was the closest I could come to for a romantic, candlelight dinner.

When Dan walked in the door, his initial surprise was quickly replaced by his wide, sexy grin, as he realized that we were alone. "Where is the kid?" he asked eagerly. We had never had the chance to be together alone since we had Lynette.

"I arranged for my mother to watch Lynette for the evening, and I prepared a wonderful, romantic evening for my husband," I purred. My heart swelled with love, and my hopes soared that we could have a wonderful evening together. Here was the man I fell in love with; the man who could sell snow to Eskimos with that smile. As soon as he wolfed down the meal, however, he announced that he was going out with the boys.

∽ 25 ∽

CHAPTER TWELVE
NEW HOME

"**M**ale company!" I yelled before I thought about it. "I made you a nice dinner. We haven't had any time alone together since we came back home, and all you can think of is male company? Dan, what is *wrong* with you?"

The reprieve was over. The rebuke was swift and sure. The punch to my shoulder made me see the stars his lovemaking didn't, and I thanked God that it wasn't my face that met his fist. And so began the cycle again. Whenever Lynette was not around, he began hitting me when we disagreed or when I questioned his actions or decisions. But I was not about to rock the boat. I told myself that it wasn't so bad. Things were moving ahead. I had to continue to ensure that I had support for my daughter.

Dan had found a job in a factory and with our combined salaries we were able to purchase a modest house. It was a small four-room house: a bedroom, living room, kitchen, and bathroom, not much bigger than the apartment above my parents' house.

It was an old-fashioned A-frame with walls that were constructed of wood planks joined together in the tongue and groove style. It had been many years, maybe decades, since it had seen paint or varnish and the floorboards, while sound, were covered in layers of dirt and grime. But it wasn't anything that a little elbow grease and a scrub brush and soap and water couldn't fix.

The house had a wraparound porch that seemed to lean into the patch of hardscrabble dirt that was the yard, and the few scraggly plants struggling to survive in the tough rocks and clay acted as support for several places on the porch. Who would ever guess that not too far in the future that same yard would later produce vegetables for us?

To the average person looking on, the house might have seemed like a run-down shack, but to me, it was like the biggest mansion. It was My Home. It was the first time I could say that. It was the first time I did not have to share a bathroom with anyone else but my husband. It was the first time that I had a bedroom door to close. Shoot, truth be told, it was the first time that I had a real bedroom.

CHAPTER THIRTEEN
CHANGE

I threw myself into the task of fixing, cleaning, painting, and organizing the house after the move. Combine this with taking care of a now crawling and very curious toddler occupied all my waking and some of my sleeping moments. There were not enough hours in the days or nights, but I had no choice. The demands of motherhood and being a working wife didn't stop just because I was tired.

If I managed to get three hours sleep each night, it was a lot. And Dan was around less and less. It hadn't taken him long to lapse back to his old ways. His financial contribution began to dwindle, and he was leaving Lynette with my mother more and more frequently in the evenings while I was at work.

While I was now making as much money as he did, we had other obligations now. We had a mortgage and utilities to pay. I was now expected to do more with less, and so I became completely engrossed in working as many hours as I could at the pizza parlor. I was now working until closing twice a week, Tuesdays and Thursdays. That meant that I worked from five in the evening until two in the morning on those days. Tired was my middle name.

Maybe that was why it took me awhile to realize that I had not had my period for a while. I had come home from working a double shift and felt the usual bone tiredness that I had now accepted as a permanent state of being. I decided that maybe a shower would help to ease the fatigue and aches and pains. I was in the rare position of being alone in the house. Dan had pulled another one of his disappearing tricks while I was at work and left the baby with my mother. Thank God she was around and didn't mind watching her grandchild from time to time. I would hate to think how else I would have been able to manage otherwise.

CHAPTER FOURTEEN

BABY?

I had just stepped out of my now sparkling shower stall. It had taken me many hours and a whole can of Comet to get it sparkling clean, but it was worth every bit of the effort. As I stepped out of the shower and reached for the towel draped over the shower curtain rod, I looked around proudly, admiring my handiwork.

The bathroom had been transformed from the damp, dank place it was when we had moved in a month before. And it really didn't take a lot. A coat of paint on the wooden planks, scrubbing and cleaning the windows and floors, and the addition of a rag rug my mother made as a house-warming present, topped off by some patchwork curtains at the window and the transformation was complete.

As I looked around, I felt a sense of pride and accomplishment. Slowly but surely I was transforming our home and our lives for the better. I looked down at the water that was glistening on my skin and decided to not rush for a change. I took my time drying off and stood to admire myself in the full-length mirror Dan had brought home from the beauty parlor. It was left over from the old stuff they took out a couple months before, when the store was renovated, but it was a nice addition to the bathroom.

It was the fullness of my breasts that I noticed first. They seemed to have acquired a fullness and roundness that I had never noticed before. Instead of looking like flat pancakes, they had taken on the rounded, full shape of a Florida orange. When I was expecting Lynette, I had been so dehydrated and malnourished that my body did not even look normal, much less get fuller.

And, as I followed the natural progression of my gaze downward, the slight bulge in my stomach jolted me. *It couldn't be. Could it?* My legs were shaking so badly they could barely take me to the bedroom. I collapsed on the bed, trying to get my mind to focus. The realization was a shock to my senses. I began to laugh, cry, shake, and shiver as I figured the weeks since my last period on my fingers. It finally dawned on me that I must have gotten pregnant on the night of our romantic dinner.

Breaking the news to Dan was going to be tricky. He was bound to think that I deliberately set out to trap him into getting pregnant again. We had just moved into the house and still had challenges with managing with one child. A second one would be a big challenge, but I was resolute that we would just have to find a way to get by.

CHAPTER FIFTEEN

RAGE

I delayed telling Dan the news of my pregnancy for another week, hoping against hope that my period would come and I could laugh off my fears. But when my menses did not arrive at the end of the week, I was forced to face the fact that I was at least two months pregnant. I would have to deliver the news. And, of course, I didn't handle it well.

I had decided that I would tell Dan in a public place, where he could not cause a scene or resort to violence. Up to that point he had never hit me in public. His ministrations were always saved for behind closed doors. I decided I would tell him on Sunday when we had our weekly trip to the Pixie Diner which was our treat with Lynette.

I had dropped the baby off at my mother's on Friday evening. I had the rare treat of a free evening off, but she was spending the weekend with my mother. We would get her on Sunday afternoon.

Dan did not stumble home until the wee hours of Saturday morning. And as usual, he was reeking of liquor. He wisely decided to sleep on the couch in the living room. When he managed to rouse himself from his drunken stupor, I reminded him that we needed to go grocery shopping. I had started to insist that he accompany me to the store, since that was the only way I got him to make a contribution to providing food for us. It being Saturday, he also had to work the afternoon shift in the beauty parlor, so even though he was hung over, we still needed to get going.

As we were leaving the house I made the mistake of asking why he abused himself so much. Maybe it was the hangover, or maybe it was because I said something he didn't want to hear, or maybe he just couldn't hold the rage back anymore. Whatever the reason, he turned around and hit me in the stomach as hard as he could.

The blow felt as if I had walked into a battering ram, and I felt as if I would never be able to catch my breath. As I doubled over, gasping for breath, I was aware of a gushing feeling in my lower abdomen. Instinctively, I started crying and screaming, "You've killed my baby!" There it was. Now he knew.

Looking around frantically to see if any of the neighbors had seen anything, Dan quickly gathered me up and took me inside to the bedroom. He was scared, but his anger had not dissipated. "What do you mean I killed your baby? Are you crazy, bitch? What baby? I don't know anything about a baby." And with that, he stormed out of the bedroom, slamming the door behind him, leaving me moaning in pain, holding my throbbing stomach.

I could hear him storming about in the living room, smashing the few belongings we had. But he stayed away from me in the bedroom, and after about an hour, I heard the front door slam shut, and I knew he had left for work.

He did not come home that night, and the next day I started passing blood. He did not come home on Sunday night either. After a day curled up in bed, rocking myself through the pains that were stabbing my abdomen, and a delirious night, I walked to the doctor's office which was four blocks away from our house. After examining me, he gave me the news that the baby was aborting.

When the doctor asked what had happened, once again I was forced to lie. I told him I had fallen down the front step after my husband left for work. Not only was I too ashamed to tell the doctor the truth, I was afraid that the police would get involved.

The doctor tried to console me by explaining that the baby was probably damaged by the fall and would not be formed correctly. "This is nature's way of taking care of these things. It's all for the best. But not to worry, you are young and you and your husband can try again after a few months." I smiled through my tears at his kind words, but I knew the truth and would have to live with it. My husband had killed our baby in a fit of rage.

CHAPTER SIXTEEN
AVAILABLE OPTIONS

Dan came home that night, but did not make an effort to come near or speak to me. I had a doctor's note that stated that I had had a miscarriage and needed 14 days off. Although my boss was not happy about the situation, he consented to giving me seven days off with pay and the other week off without pay. My mother agreed to take Lynette for a week to give me a chance to rest and recuperate. It also gave me a chance to think about my position and to contemplate my available options.

Lynette was a chubby, happy toddler whose only care in the world was being hugged and tickled by her Nana and Mommy. As with any normal child entering the terrible twos, she could be willful sometimes, testing the boundaries of tolerance and patience. I had always tried to shield her from any and all harm, and Dan, for all his faults, had so far never let her see his abuse of me. I also never said a bad word about him to her. But I began to feel terrified for my child. While I kept telling myself that Dan would never hurt her, I couldn't be sure that she wouldn't get hurt in one of his abusive attacks on me. I knew that I had to find a way to get us out of the predicament.

In the 1960s in Midwest America, it was a disgrace to be divorced. Wives were expected to "grin and bear it" and submit to their husbands' will and wishes. It was not accepted that you would leave your husband because he hit you. Many "decent, respectable gentlemen" beat their wives and children and boasted about it to their friends and colleagues. But you did not get divorced. I didn't want to get a divorce. So I continued to live with Dan in a marriage that was a sham; a face card and pretense for the outside world. He became more and more abusive as the weeks passed, flying off the handle and slapping me at the slightest little thing. He now took care to only slap me in the back of my head or on my legs. Places where he felt he would do little damage and where there would be no obvious marks.

The more he abused me, the more the tension in the air grew when we were both in a room together. It was so thick you could cut it with a knife. In my mind, there was always the 800-pound gorilla lurking in the corner. "You killed my baby! You hit me and killed my baby!" And a cold fist increased its icy grip on my heart. We lived like this for a few more months before the bottom fell out completely.

CHAPTER SEVENTEEN
CONFESSION TO FAMILY

The day started with my usual routine. I woke at 5:00 when Lynette climbed over the railing of the crib, as was her practice now that we had finally managed to get one for her and she no longer slept in our bed with us, and pulled on my hair. "Mommy, I'm hungry. I need my cereal, Mommy," she demanded in her high-pitched, squeaky, toddler voice. Not baby talk anymore, but not big kid voice yet.

As I eased out from under the blanket, Dan burrowed deeper under the covers. He had not come home until the wee hours and was suffering the aftereffects of his evening indulging in an overdose of riotous living. I quickly gathered Lynette up as she headed toward his side of the bed and bundled her out to the kitchen. Soon she was settled at the table eating her bowl of Rice Krispies and milk, chattering away in her special language, describing the fairies that had populated her dreams the night before.

We passed an hour of Mommy and me time before Dan stumbled out of the bedroom, heading straight for the coffee that I had already brewed. He poured his mug of coffee and left the pot on the counter, without even a backward glance at the ring that was being scorched into the Formica countertop. As he headed for the bathroom still carrying his mug of coffee, he mumbled that he needed a clean ironed shirt for work.

Being a dutiful wife, I got the iron and ironing board from the hallway cupboard and searched the laundry basket for one of Dan's work shirts. As I stood over the ironing board, waiting for the iron to heat up, I happened to notice a business card in the shirt's pocket. I must have overlooked it when I did the laundry at the local Laundromat. As

I fished the card out of the pocket, I noticed that it was not the usual business card. But instead, it seemed to be some sort of advertising card. As I turned it over and examined it closer, my stomach churned as I swallowed back the nausea that threatened to engulf me. The advertising was for a private men's club where, as the fine print stated, *"men can meet other men in a discreet atmosphere."*

I was rooted to the spot where I stood, not even noticing that the iron was lying facedown on the shirt pocket. I looked up when Dan came into the room, and it was then that I smelled the odor of burning fabric. It registered on my consciousness just as Dan rushed across the room toward me and grabbed the card from my hand.

The fist blow to my face sent me sprawling to the floor, the ironing board and iron collapsing in a heap. The stars and lights that flashed before my eyes blinked like the Christmas tree that was erected in the city square. But instead of staying down, I immediately jumped to my feet and without even hesitating, I grabbed a large glass vase from the dish drainer and swung with all my might at his head.

The sound of the glass impacting with Dan's head had barely registered on my brain before I scooped up a bewildered Lynette in my arms and bolted out the door. I did not stop running until I reached my mother's house.

I was finally forced to face the fact that my husband had crossed over the line. I had to confess to my family that his behavior, past and present, showed that it was not safe for me or my child to be around him. He had not hesitated to slug me in front of my daughter, and I had no confidence that he would not soon turn on her as well. This had to be the last time he ever hit me.

I went to the courthouse and filed a restraining order and eviction notice against him. He moved out of the house the next day, after he was served with the papers at the beauty parlor, and left Lynette and me to fend for ourselves.

CHAPTER EIGHTEEN

THE AFTERMATH

Watching Dan walk out the door with his meager belongings piled into the battered car he still had from Florida, my heart was breaking, not only for myself, but more so for my daughter, Lynette. I had such high hopes for us as a family. Instead, at the age of 21, I was a cowed and battered, about to be divorced, single mother with a house mortgage and bills to pay. And thinking about the bills reminded me that I had just enough time to get Lynette to my mother and make it to the pizza parlor for my shift.

Our little girl was three years old when Dan left me. And for quite a while after he was gone she would ask and ask, "Where did Daddy go? When is he coming back?" I tried to get her to understand that her daddy was not coming back. When the questions didn't stop, I finally relented and took her to where he was staying in a small town nearby and ask if he would see her. He grudgingly agreed, but paid very little attention to her even though she was crazy about him.

After the visit, Dan showed no interest in his child and never came to visit her. God forgive me, but as my daughter grew and began asking questions about him, I always told her he had moved so far away that he could not come and see her. Of course, I should not have lied. One day she saw his name in our local paper and became furious with me. *"Why have you lied to me for all these years?"* she yelled. The fact of the matter was that I felt she would be hurt if she realized he lived so close and had never even called her. When she was older she went to see him. He basically ignored her, leaving her scared and angry. That ended her desire to know him.

He married again, and his next wife suffered the same abuse as

I did. She was beaten terribly on more than one occasion, and even went to the police station once to file a report. She later withdrew the complaint and committed suicide. I have heard that he married again a couple of times after that.

While I regret lying to my daughter, I do not regret shielding her from Dan. Only a coward and a monster beat up women and abandon his children. I'm sure unless he has turned to God by now, he will burn in hell for all the things he has done.

CHAPTER NINETEEN
LUNCH IN THE MOUNTAINS

As the bus wound its way across the mountains, we passed through towns with names like Anchovy and Ramble and finally reached our destination, an old plantation in the hills, overlooking the town of Whitehouse and the dazzling blue Caribbean Sea. This was to be our stop for lunch.

The main house, which was built in the Georgian style, was part of a working plantation perched high up in the mountains. It was surrounded by a scattering of small buildings and sheds and sat in scenery that could only be described as breathtaking. Everywhere was the sound of birds chirping. We would later learn that they were the native green parrots indigenous to the parish of Westmoreland.

The interior of the house was immaculate, with the vast rooms furnished with highly polished mahogany antiques that stood proudly on glistening dark wood floors. Old Persian and Oriental rugs provided the finishing touch.

The working plantation was the home of Dr. Cyril Ball, his wife Marjorie, and their young daughter Daynee-Anne. Dr. Ball was a friendly, soft-spoken Englishman who was the local doctor and had his surgery clinic on the main street of the town. His wife Marjorie was a beautiful, exotic Jamaican woman who embodied the country's motto which we had learned was "Out of Many, One People." While her features had a distinctly oriental cast, her mocha skin color spoke to a not-too-distant African ancestor. Later on, when I got to know her better, I would learn that her mother was Chinese and her father a black man.

Mrs. Ball, or Marge, as she preferred to be called, was a superb hostess who effortlessly made everybody feel at home. As we disembarked the bus, we were greeted with crystal goblets of ice-cold water as well as fruit punch and rum punch for those brave enough to try the local concoction whose key ingredient was 150 proof white rum.

Lunch was a buffet laid out on long trestle tables on the verandah that wrapped around the entire main building. The tables were laden with a sumptuous feast of spicy "jerk" pork, roasted beef, and baked chicken, stewed oxtails, curried lobsters and succulent garlic shrimp in a rich coconut sauce, a wide array of vegetables, a delicious rice dish cooked in coconut milk with red beans, the creamiest mashed potatoes I had ever tasted, macaroni and cheese, a mixed salad of lettuce, red and white cabbage, shredded carrots, cucumbers, tomatoes, and enough fruits, some of which I had never heard of, to keep the Chinese army scurvy-free for a year.

After lunch, Dr. Ball invited those in the group who could still move and who wished to get some exercise before the bus ride back to the ship to hike in the bushes to check out a cave nearby that was said to have once housed first the Arawak Indians who lived on the island before Christopher Columbus's arrival and then the Maroons, runaway slaves who fought and eventually defeated the British army. While Mel eagerly jumped at the chance to do something active and was soon leading the pack, I opted to stay back at the house and lounge on the verandah, looking out at the village and the sea. It also gave me the opportunity to talk with Marge.

CHAPTER TWENTY

MEETING MARGE

At first, we just lay in two of the old mahogany and rattan lounge chairs that lined the section of the verandah that looked out over the village and the sea. Though the house was set back more than a mile from the main village square, it was perched high enough that it gave a perfect 360-degree view of the town.

Whitehouse was a little fishing village on the south coast of Jamaica, really not a place where I would have picked to go. The village was only a few blocks long with one or two streets leading to the sea. Along the road were small, handmade shops constructed from leftover wood and tin. At the end of the roads leading to the sea, fishing boats large and small, were docked, waiting for the day they would go to sea for another catch.

As she caught the direction of my gaze, Marge explained to me that the boats were all made from cottonwood trees that had been cut and hollowed out to make the crafts. They were all painted in different colors and against the blue Caribbean Sea, it was very joyful to see them bobbing up and down with the surf.

Since she didn't seem averse to talking with me, I decided to try to learn as much as I could about the island from Marge. In answer to my query about how she spent her days, Marge was quick to assure me that she was no rich, pampered wife. In fact, she was a hardworking, building contractor.

At present, she was in the midst of navigating the government bureaucratic maze to get the necessary paperwork, plans, permits, and approvals to proceed to develop the hundreds of acres of rugged coastline and mountain property in Whitehouse that she had recently inherited from her father.

She was marketing the real estate to Jamaicans overseas and hoped to establish what she envisioned as an all-inclusive, safe, luxury, gated community on the seaside portion of the property, and country homes on the mountainside part of the property. She pictured this part of the development attracting young persons who wanted a rental or time share property as an investment for future income.

"A seaside lot on the water would be perfect for you as a retirement place to get away from the cold during the wintertime," she teased. "Anytime you're ready to retire to the tropics, even for a few weeks, let me know," she declared, while proceeding to fill me in on the details of the villas and apartments she would like to build.

As she described her vision to me, I couldn't help but wonder what it would be like to live with the sea in my backyard.

But, in a flash, the daydream was ended when the hikers returned, and the tour group prepared to depart for the drive to Montego Bay and the return to the cruise ship. The girls had stayed on board to swim and play games that the cruise line has for the younger set. It would be nice to tell them of our trip and how excited I was about this beautiful island. As Marge wished us bon voyage and we hugged good-bye, she reminded me with a cheeky wink, "Remember, if you ever want to give up the cold Midwest for the warm tropics, don't hesitate to call."

I was sincerely touched by her warmth and kindness and assured her that I would keep in touch. We had exchanged telephone numbers. Even though telephone service was mostly nonexistent for most residents in rural Jamaica, because her husband was a doctor, they had the luxury of a working landline phone.

As the bus winded its way down the hill to Whitehouse and along the coast road down to Montego Bay, I felt in my heart that I had truly made a friend that day and without knowing when, was sure that I would return someday.

The drive back to the ship, while it seemed shorter, was still a few hours. As I stared out the bus window, I was engrossed in my own thoughts, vaguely aware of Mel as he kept asking what Marge meant by coming to the tropics to live. But I really wasn't in the mood to talk and continued to stare out the window, not seeing anything; instead, I found myself thinking once again of the past.

CHAPTER TWENTY-ONE

A NEW LIFE

I was so scared after the divorce from Dan while trying to keep a place to live, raise a child on my own, and work. As I worked the counter at the pizza parlor, it was almost impossible to keep my mind on the job when my thoughts kept wandering. How would I pay the bills? Was slinging pizza at night my destiny? What if Lynette gets sick? Suppose I get sick? How would we manage? I had to find the answers. I decided to talk with my brother about my possibilities.

My brother Dennis was nine years older than me and had always been my rock. Sometimes I think he has been the only stable factor in my life. He was my hero and always tried to be there when I needed something. In my eyes, he stood for everything that was good and decent. When he turned eighteen, Dennis joined the U.S. Navy, and the day he left was one of the most devastating times of my life. Everything I knew to be solid was leaving. I was left to fend for myself when it came to family problems. No one to run to and no one to tell my troubles to.

Dennis was deployed to the Panama Canal Zone and was trained to be a sonar technician. Every day I would run to the mailbox to see if we got a letter from him. He always encouraged me in his letters and, really, that was the only time I ever received praise or encouragement from anyone. It kept me going, with all the drinking and money problems at home getting worse and coping with the rich kids at school who snubbed me. I wondered if I would ever make it out of the hellhole my life was fast becoming.

Four years after his enlistment, my brother returned to our home. He joined the Delaware County Sheriff's Department, and it seemed his life was going somewhere. He would drive up in his sheriff's car, wearing his brown and tan uniform with his brown ten-gallon hat, and sit on our front porch, telling tales about the criminals that he was in pursuit of. It sounded so exciting and adventurous that I would repeat the stories over and over to my friends. I know they got sick of hearing about my big brother, but I didn't care.

My parents also felt the sun rose and set on my brother. When he would drive up in his sheriff's car, we would all have the same happy smile on our faces. He had become the one to believe in, and he was making them very proud, to say the least.

Then something happened to me deep down in my spirit. It became a knowing, as if it was all I could imagine, a constant thought, a dream, really not anything I can describe.

At fourteen I knew that I was to follow my brother's footsteps and become a cop. The funny thing about this thinking was that there was no such thing as a female cop in the mid-'50s. This was still a time when women wore only dresses, no pants or jeans in school, and definitely it was a man's world. But it didn't matter to me. I now had my mind set, and that was that! I know from that time on, I walked a little taller, I became braver, and I knew where I was going to head—out of the house of horrors and into the light.

I began reading everything I could get my hands on about police procedure, criminal investigation, and anything that related to police work. I would make trips to the city police department, ask questions, and talk to the chief of police whenever I could find him. I let them know that I wanted to be appointed to the department. This was on my mind constantly and all that I could think of. I was seventeen when I kept bugging the front office.

My persistence finally paid off. At the age of nineteen, the chief invited me to attend the city's very first police school. It would last eight weeks and was going to be a new concept in police work. At that time, young police recruits were usually given a uniform and a gun and sent on the street without any type of training. You learned from other seasoned officers, or you got yourself into a lot of trouble. Chief Carey wanted to change that image and send officers out with some "school learning."

I was so excited! The training was exactly what I wanted. The school consisted of classroom and field training, including the gun range. For some reason, I was a natural on the gun range, hitting the chest area every time. The sound of the bullets and the excitement of it all was quite an adrenalin rush. I did well on the tests each week and finished second in the class of forty.

However, I was not appointed to the department. I was only nineteen, and the department required that you be at least twenty-one. Chief Carey stated at graduation that had I been twenty-one, he would have appointed me the first woman in the Muncie Police Department. I was walking on air. I was within reach of achieving my dream of following in my brother's footsteps. I just had to wait out the next two years.

It was at that time that I met Dan, and maybe it was my disappointment at not being appointed that made me deviate from my plan. Who knows? He was my first boyfriend, and when I started dating him at eighteen, he looked like the answer to all my problems. When I met him the year before, something clicked with him and after dating for a year, he gave me a diamond ring. I felt loved at the time, something I had never experienced before.

It is really strange how your life can be arranged by a mere thing you call love. Young and inexperienced, green and really stupid, I gave my heart away, only to have it nearly kill me later.

Well, it was now time to get back on track. I called my brother and asked him to stop by later that evening. I would discuss with Dennis what he felt were my chances of getting into the police department. As I watched my brother walk into the pizza parlor that evening, I couldn't help but smile. I think my hero worship started at the same time that I experienced fear, trust, and the power of faith and prayer, all at the same time. It was when our family was caught in a blizzard when I was seven.

CHAPTER TWENTY-TWO

TWINKLE, TWINKLE, LITTLE STAR

The blizzard raged in the flatlands of Kansas. This may well be the worst place in the world when the dark clouds of winter blow. The flat terrain of Kansas makes for a perfect land of howling winds without anything to stop them. Summer dust storms and winter blizzards are common and very dangerous. I was as scared as I had ever been in my short life. My father was driving without any type of visibility. You have heard of occasions when you could not see your hand in front of your face. Well, this was the real thing.

It was getting toward night and between the darkness and the blowing snow we all felt trapped and knew that we would be found dead if we did not find shelter soon. My mother began to hyperventilate, which was a sure sign to me that she knew we would not make it out alive. The old 1936 Ford was giving it all it could, but just the same, as it chugged along, we would hardly go a few feet before my sixteen-year-old brother Dennis would have to get out and push. He soon had to sit on the hood of the car and keep the windshield clear from the blowing snow.

If a child of seven can sense death, it was very clear to me that we were doomed and headed for a white winter's grave. We were going to die. My mother was beginning to panic, and when your mother starts to panic and cry, you get the picture real fast that you and your family were not going to make it through the cold and snowy night.

I wondered what I could do to stop the march into the darkness of death. I decided to pray. Thing is, I had never heard a prayer in my seven years of life. The only time I heard the Lord's name in my home it was in vain.

"Twinkle, twinkle, little star, how I wonder what you are?" As strange as that seems, it was the only prayer I knew. It was only later in life that I realized that was not a prayer but a nursery rhyme. To a child, wishing and praying seemed to go together. Besides, my only hope was the fact that it might reach heaven's gates.

My family had been caught that evening on the flatlands of Kansas as we were heading for Indiana after a year of living in Colorado. We had moved out west because my father's health was deteriorating and he had been laid off from the foundry in Muncie, my birth town, a small Midwest city in Indiana.

As I kept repeating my prayer over and over, far in the distance we could see a flicker of light. It was almost like a mirage at first, so very far away. This was the first thing we had seen for hours, so my father headed for the light. By this time, we were not following a road, just the flicker of light which turned out to be the neon light of a small motel. In the 1940s, the motels in the American heartland were small cottages, and although this one looked a little shabby and run-down, we didn't give a hoot. The moment we pulled near, they flicked out the light. We piled out of the car and went inside to the desk.

Inquiring for a room, the man at the desk said there was no vacancy. "Okay, we'll sleep on the floor here by the desk," my father informed him. The desk clerk looking at four, cold, and desperate people, and agreed to give us the last small room he had left. It was the best-looking room I had ever seen, even though my mom said she wondered if the place had bugs. We were so tired and weary from the trip, though, that we all piled into one bed and slept as the winds of the blizzard blew outside.

Although the next morning we could not find our car which had been buried in snow, I knew my prayer had been answered no matter how simple it had been. I knew in my heart that God had heard, and

He had watched over us. Many years later, my brother said he never understood why there was one room left and that perhaps the man was going to sleep there, but I knew that it was a magical thing that God had performed, a miracle, one of many I would see throughout my life.

CHAPTER TWENTY-THREE

COLORADO

The year before, my mother and I had traveled by train from Indiana to Colorado to join my father and brother who had been living in Colorado for six months while my father looked for work. Back in Indiana, his health problems with ulcers and miserable sinus problems were getting the best of him.

My father's sister, my aunt Mable, had moved to Colorado a few years earlier with her Italian husband. Aunt Mable was six foot three, a big lady, and her husband Tony was a short little guy. They looked comical together, especially when Mable would wear high heels. My father was impressed with her and what she was telling him about the West. Move west, move west she would say, and all your health problems will be solved.

The train ride to Colorado was as exciting as the thought of going to an amusement park. No, I had neither been to an amusement park nor been on a train before, but this had to be the highlight of a little six-year-old's life. Friends had packed us a picnic basket with chicken and bread and butter for the trip. I know we were not out of Indiana before we started eating the lunch. To this very day, I can remember the wonderful taste of that lunch. I have never been able to duplicate the taste of that fried chicken and warm bread and butter.

The train ride took three days, and as we would go around curves of the tracks, I could see the engine of the train puffing smoke and rocking on the tracks, while the coal soot and smoke drifted into the open windows of our coach. After the first blush of excitement wore off, the train ride became long and boring with seats that did not command comfort. But, eventually, we reached our destination.

When we arrived at the station in Denver, we were tired and dirty, but I was glad we had finally made it. I was the first to see my brother and father and waved as hard as I could and ran to them. My mother went over to my father and attempted to give him a kiss, but he jerked away from her. She was left standing with a sad-looking face, an expression I had seen and would see many more times.

My father had an old, battered Ford that he had bought for the trip from Indiana. Now, my mother and I piled into the car for the trip to our home. To our "cabin in the sky," as my father put it. The trip to our new house was two hours from Denver, and I kept staring out the window at the big mountains, some with snowcaps. This was nothing like the cornfields of Indiana that roll on forever. A land that was dotted with red barns and cows feeding in the pastures. I felt like I was entering Never-Never Land.

CHAPTER TWENTY-FOUR

IDAHO SPRINGS

The closest town to where we lived was located three miles be-low us. Idaho Springs was an old mining town with hot springs and a river running through the middle of town. It had an old "iron horse" locomotive that had run on the tracks in the 1800s sitting in the middle of town. A little picture-postcard town in a valley with large, snowcapped mountains all around. The road to Idaho Springs was a rugged road with mountains each way I looked.

When we approached the cabin from the main road, it seemed as if there were no roads to turn on. I was sure my father didn't really know where he was going and was going to shoot right down the cliff. *Oh, this is it! We are going to wreck and go right down the mountainside.* But we soon came to the turnoff which was a narrow, bumpy lane that ran straight down from the main road and was just big enough to accom-modate one car. When it came into view, I was relieved to see the little cabin with a red front door.

The cabin was sitting on a carved-out side of a mountain with a very little yard and a small place to park the car. The back side of the roof touched the mountain. It was the real deal as mountain cabins went. It had been built possibly 100 years before, and had four rooms and an awesome view of Pike's Peak with pine trees as far as the eye could see. The mountain had snowy peaks, and even as a child, I knew it was one of the most beautiful sights in the world.

But as our newly reunited family got settled, I sensed that all was not well. While my father loved it in Colorado, my mom quickly be-came very lonely. She was becoming very depressed, and the deeper the depression, the more she would drink. She would go around the cabin and sing a song that she made up. It went "Pine trees, pine trees, pine trees, pine trees" and she sang it to the tune of "Auld Lang Syne." I would laugh at the song but soon realized that she was becoming very depressed and lonely.

The cabin was heated by a woodstove in the middle of the living room. As winter approached, the cabin was icy cold as winds whistled through the cracks. We cooked on a woodstove in the kitchen, and, weather permitting, I would play on the roof of the cabin as it was easy to access from the side of the mountain. At night, I would fall asleep to the howling of coyotes nearby and try to remember the warmth of my bed in Indiana where bears and coyotes were not a worry.

I had no playmates my age, just forest and wilderness as my playground. I had not been able to bring my little doll or any other playthings on the train, so I took my mother's mop and made a doll by using lipstick to draw a face on the mop. I named her "Mopsy." She was taller than me and was my constant companion. She would hop along beside me everywhere I would go. Of course, she had my loving assistance, and at times, I really believed she understood everything I said to her. One day I came home from school to find that Mopsy was missing. I searched for her until my mother told me that she had used her to mop the floor. That was the end of Mopsy. I was heartbroken.

I was enrolled in the first grade at the local elementary school and each day, walking to school was terrifying. I was always afraid I would meet up with a bear or porcupine along the path. My brother would tease me about all the things that lived in the forest, and that would send me into further panic. Big brothers love to tease little sisters, but I did not realize it at the time in my childish innocence. I was extra scared, and going to school, I would try to walk as fast as my legs could carry me, attempting to keep up with my brother who was fifteen years old and a very fast walker.

The vast wilderness in the Arapahoe Forest and the downhill walk to school would scare me out of my little head at times. In the winter, when the river was frozen, we would walk across it since it was shorter way to get to school if we went across it. I would slip and slide down the river past the old mill wheel to the other side of town where the school was located. The cracking of the ice below my feet as I hurried along only added to my worries.

In Colorado, I began seeing a difference in my parents. My father was becoming an alcoholic, and my mother was not far behind him. They, along with Aunt Mable, would drink liquor all day, and by evening, they would be staggering all over the place. Aunt Mable would become filled with laughter when she drank, but my father would start out with a bad attitude, and as he drank, would then slip into needing sleep, perhaps a nod and a nap, and once he woke up, move into the mean and hateful bashing phase as he continued to drink himself into oblivion.

Living in the cold little cabin was really getting to my mom. She had left all her family, sisters, brothers, and friends behind in Indiana. When I think back on this period of my life, I realize what a brave and courageous woman my mother was. It would take an army to make me put up with what she took from my dad.

I hated my life and wanted someone to rescue me from this terrible world of drink and drunk. My brother was the only stabilizing factor, really my hero at times, and was always there when I needed something. Nothing seemed to be going right, and I didn't even have Mopsy to talk to any longer. I spent many days and nights alone while my parents were out drinking at bars or sleeping off a drunk. I sank into a make-believe world of fairies and beautiful gardens where flowers grew in abundance. I would cut out models in catalogs and use them as paper dolls. I would talk to myself as I walked to school, pretending to have someone with me.

My father's health was deteriorating, and his drinking was out of control. Right before Christmas and my seventh birthday, my father collapsed over the steering wheel of his car. He was rushed to the nearby hospital, where we learned that his stomach had perforated and burst. He lost a lot of blood and was in danger of dying. The doctors removed most of his stomach, attaching what was left to the upper part of his chest. He was near death for days.

I found out my father was in the hospital when my mother and brother came into the large room of our cabin where I was sitting on the floor playing with paper dolls that I had cut out of a catalog. They had a worried look on their faces. "We need to tell you that we will not be having Christmas this year," my mother said, and handed me two wrapped gifts. "We have to go to the hospital and stay with your father because he is very ill."

What? Not have Christmas! How could that be? In my world of fairies and beautiful people, there was no skipping Christmas. I pitched a fit, screaming and crying, and told them *I WOULD NOT GO!* "Santa Clause will not be able to find me in Denver in a hospital."

It was the first time that my world came crashing down when my brother coldly shut me up. "It's time you learn the truth about Santa. He doesn't exist. It's just a story," Dennis told me.

I was totally crushed and cried and cried. I had believed in Santa Clause so strongly, and now my dreams of fairies and Santa were gone. To this day, I begin to get depressed at Christmas, usually when I take the first decoration out of the packed-away boxes. I have a deep crying in my soul during the holidays, and it does not end until Christmas is over.

Mother told me that we would have to go back to Indiana as soon as my father was able to drive. He was still recuperating from the stomach surgery, which would make the trip more stressful and dangerous than ever when we started our journey in late February 1945. That is how we ended up in the blizzard that nearly finished us off.

CHAPTER TWENTY-FIVE

BACK TO INDIANA

We made it back to Indiana, but we were four homeless people. Our home had been sold when we left for Colorado, and in the mid-'40s, there was a housing crisis with all the boys coming home from World War II and starting families. My mother, dad, and brother moved in with my grandmother when we returned to Indiana. I didn't move with them. The house was too small for all of us, so I was given to my aunt Ruby for a time.

Aunt Ruby was my mother's oldest sister and one of the dizziest dames I had ever seen. She had high morals and was a religious lady who treated me well and made sure I went to church, although, she seemed to be in a different world all the time. Sometimes she would go to use the phone, dial, and then forget who she was calling. Her home was within walking distance to the Burris School in Muncie. That was how I came to be enrolled in the school.

Burris was an elite school whose students came from families that were very wealthy and influential. They included the children of the founder of Ball State University, the university in our city. Some of the children were brought to school in limousines, and most lived in mansions in West Wood. West Wood had houses that only my imagination could picture with most being three stories tall with vast, beautifully manicured lawns and driveways that looked like avenues. I longed to see inside the houses and longed to have a place that I could call home.

At first, I was enrolled in second grade. I was one of the biggest and tallest kids in the class, but was beginning to catch on. But for some ungodly reason, the school authorities decided to double promote me. I was skipped two grades to fourth grade. That was when school got rough for me. What a big change from grade one. When the teacher would write something on the board, it looked strange because I only knew how to print, not do cursive writing. I would lay my head down on the desk because I could not follow along.

Meanwhile, things got worse in my living situation. I left Aunt Ruby's house and moved back with my parents and brother, but still attended Burris.

My grandfather died and the home place was available for our family, so there was now room for me at home. My family reunited, and we moved into my mother's homestead. It was in a neighborhood of houses built in the 1920s except for our house which had been in my mother's family since the turn of the century. It was a big, old, two-story with two bedrooms down and four rooms up. My widowed cousin lived upstairs with her two daughters, and we took the downstairs.

My bedroom ended up being in the dining room, which was okay with me. At least it was warm, and I didn't have to worry about wild animals. We shared one bathroom with my cousin, and the house was so old and rotted that the toilet was about to fall into the basement. A large hole near the toilet was gapping and had, of all things, mushrooms growing near the toilet.

The house was heated with a coal furnace, and my job was to make sure the big hog had coal in it at all times. The coal was delivered by truck and slid down a coal chute to a bin. I would pick up the coal shovel and with all my might, deliver it to the fire. Sometimes I waited too long and the fire would go out. When that happened, the house would become freezing cold in an hour or less. Keeping that sucker fed was a dirty job, and sometimes we would not have enough coal to stoke the big old furnace.

Mom would sometimes joke by saying we could chop the furniture up and use it for heat. But we never had to resort to such desperate measures. When we didn't have money for coal, usually we would walk along the railroad and find pieces of coal that fell from the coal trains. And once in a while when things got really rough, we would go to the coal yard and "help ourselves" to some coal. This was always on the sly and only when we became so desperate that we had no other way to keep warm.

CHAPTER TWENTY-SIX

LIFE IN MUNCIE

It was the early '50s and things seemed to be getting worse in my world. We were as poor as a family could be, my father being laid off most of the time from the foundry where he worked, and my mother did everything she could to make ends meet. The foundry where my dad worked was a hot hole with big furnaces to melt iron and make cores for auto engines. My father would come home hot, tired, and dirty each evening. Then the drinking would begin, and somehow, he made it to work the next day.

I need only close my eyes, and I can immediately imagine the smell in our house, a combination of old, dirty foundry, booze, and train engine smoke. Yes, I was from the wrong side of the tracks, and as funny as it seems, the tracks were beside our house. The train would shake the old windows and wake me. The windows were always dirty, and the paper drapes at the windows were torn and taped together in places to make them last a little longer. My mother did everything she could to put food on the table. She would walk along the railroad gathering wild strawberries and cooked dandelion greens to supplement our meager menu which mostly consisted of beans. Most of the money in the household was spent on wine and beer.

My dad was drunk most of the time when he was home, either sitting in his chair drinking, sleeping it off, or yelling at me for some unknown reason. At times he would grab his belt and beat me for reasons I never understood. I never knew what would trigger his outrage, so I lived in fear most of the time. But there were times I got my revenge. Sometimes I would get so mad at him when he wasn't looking I would pour out half of his hidden wine jug and refill it with water.

My reasoning was at least he would not get as drunk as usual. But this would usually mean another beating, sometimes in the head with his heavy shoe. My brother would try to stop him, and many times I would run to him for a shield. Sometimes Dad would beat my mother, and I would try to get between them, thinking that it was better that he beat me rather than have him beat her. One time during a violent argument, he blooded her face, and I fainted at the sight of her blood.

Mother was becoming an alcoholic too, telling me she had to drink with my father to be able to tolerate his drinking. She had one great personality when she was not drinking and everyone loved her. Her pet name was Tay, but I never did know why she got that name or who pinned it on her.

My mother was kind and good-hearted and would give her last cent if someone asked for it. Once, during a storm, an old hobo came to our back door asking for food. We barely had enough for ourselves, but my mother gave him something to eat and a hot cup of tea. Guess the word got around that our house was a place you could at least get a piece of bread, because after that, others would come to us when they were in need. It always scared me in a way to see these "nomads," but as poor as we were, mom would always find something to feed them.

I attended Burris School in Muncie, from second grade to my high school graduation. Since most of the kids came from rich and influential families, they all seemed to have an attitude problem. They never had anything to do with the kids that came in the south side door of the school. We were considered "trash." You needed a tough shell to not be one of "them" and still hold your head up.

My schoolmates' parents were bankers, college presidents, doctors, lawyers, and judges. The kids I went to school with lived in mansions and their families had cars, something we never had. And then there were a few like me who lived on the wrong side of the tracks. My dad took the bus to work, and if we needed to go somewhere, we walked or took the bus. My clothes were handed down to me by an older cousin, and I'm sure I looked funny and strange wearing such adult clothes. I pretended not to notice that the "in crowd" always had a good laugh over my attire.

Our home was filled with drinking, fighting, cursing, and the smell of alcohol to the point that we were becoming outcasts. The house was in deep need of repair, we had paper drapes, bare floors, and furniture that people had given us, and the aroma of wine drifted through the house. Our home was not a place where I could bring friends. It was not a place where other parents would allow their children to visit. I felt ashamed and started telling big stories about how successful my family was. I'm sure no one believed me, but at least it made me feel better.

But all that changed at fourteen when I decided that I would try to follow my brother's steps and become a cop. That was all I could talk about to my friends. I knew that in order to become a cop, I would have to become strong, have high moral standards, and be fair and honest. It became a dream to let myself think that I would ever become anything near my brother's status.

As a first step, I started to pay closer attention to my personal hygiene and began counseling my friends who were getting involved in immoral activities, such as smoking, drinking, and having sex. I never smoked or drank and vowed not to engage in sex before marriage. Many of my friends today thank me for keeping them out of trouble and advising them to stay on track.

One of my best friends, Elaine, who I spent most of my time with, was a beautiful girl. She was younger than I by a few years, but for some reason, we clicked as friends and would go everywhere together. Her family was well off, not rich, but had a very nice house and a lake cottage. They were so kind to me and would invite me to the lake cottage most weekends. I dearly loved to be around water, and swimming was one of my passions. I still would rather be swimming than anything else.

One day at the lakes I found a pack of cigarettes in a pair of jeans that were hanging in the bathroom. There was no mistake that the jeans belonged to Elaine. I tore into her with a vengeance that only a parent could do. I yelled at her for over twenty minutes. I must have scared her real good because she never smoked the rest of her life.

Elaine married young and left me stranded. I missed my constant companion. She did, however, come to Jamaica in later years to help with the ministry. She had divorced after twenty-five years of marriage and birthing three beautiful girls.

CHAPTER TWENTY-SEVEN

THE TEENAGE YEARS

At the end of fourth grade, I became very ill. My parents were deep into their downward alcoholic spiral, and I was near death before they realized how sick I was. By then, I had a raging fever of 105 degrees, and when I started talking out of my head, they knew that I was one sick little kid. They rushed me to the hospital immediately.

Seems I had come down with rheumatic fever, mononucleosis, and a kidney infection all at the same time. Penicillin was new to the medical world, and so every four hours, around the clock, I was given a shot of the medicine. This went on for over a month, and I believe to this day, that is what saved my life.

Our local doctor, Dr. Young, would come to our house after I was released from the hospital and give me the injections. He was a wonderful doctor and made house calls through the 1950s. He was a very pleasant man, and I always looked forward to having him visit me except for the shots. He gave me an old, needleless syringe, and I would pretend to give my big rag doll, Janie, shots all the time. I was confined to a wheelchair for the entire summer and gained a lot of weight from being inactive for so long. The weight would stay with me during my early teens.

I returned to school after the holidays, a chubby, unattractive pre-teen wearing hand-me-down clothes from an older cousin. My mother never taught me to wash my hair or any other good grooming habits. She had mentioned a few times when she was drunk, that when she was expecting me, she did not want a girl. Perhaps that explains why there was no name on my birth certificate. I discovered this when, as an adult, I attempted to apply for a passport. When I went to city hall

to get a copy of my birth certificate, there was some problem in locating it. When a clerk finally located it, there was no name recorded on it; only the word "female" was on the document. I had to convince the clerk to change it to my given name, Katherine.

My mother began having a weight problem, so she asked Dr. Young for something to help her lose weight. He started giving her Disoxin, known today as speed, but at that time, it was a diet pill commonly prescribed by doctors for their female patients. Since I was also overweight, Momama began giving it to me to lose weight.

Man, not only did I lose weight, I became addicted to the pills. I could not function without the pills which were given to us by the doctor free-of-charge and he gave us as many as we wanted. So here I am a drug addict, not knowing anything about addiction, only trusting the good doctor for another round of pills. I was developing into a young woman, but at least I was entering my teens with a trim figure.

PART TWO

CHAPTER ONE

LIFE AS A POLICE OFFICER

My life took on purpose and meaning the day I put on my uniform. Now I would be doing what I had dreamed and longed for. I was appointed as one of the city's first policewomen along with a second woman. This was front-page news, two women appointed to the Muncie Police Department, along with eight men. In the beginning, every move we made was watched by news media and the public. It would become common later on to be in the media spotlight. Women police were a rare item at that time.

My partner, Jeanie, was as different from me as night from day. She had a degree from Ball State University, and we were partners in the early years of our career. She drank with the male officers and seemed to fit in with their ways. She was always nice to me, but we were as far apart as North to South when it came to our opinions. Somehow, the first years of our assignments together, though, we were able to keep our cool and not let our different personalities get in the way of our police work. For that I'm very thankful.

We were assigned the South Walnut Street beat. I was so green and stupid and completely lacking when it came to street smarts. The seasoned officers, when they talked to us, would always say, "Street smarts do not come from a book. It comes from years of experience working the beat."

One day as I was walking the beat with a seasoned officer, we walked by a car parked in a tow away zone outside the Top Hat Cigar Store. I was about to have it towed when the officer took me to the side. "Let's you and me have a talk. Let me explain and give you some brotherly advice," he said. "We let him park there; we don't bother him." Later, I learned that the police were not only ignoring the tow away zone but the gambling that was going on in the back room of the cigar store. I vowed to stop such activities.

A few days later, I put a call in to a couple of officers and led my first raid on the Top Hat Cigar Store. This was a bold tactic because I had never even been on a raid, let alone led one. In the back room, the men at the gambling tables were some of the city's most important persons. We called for a car and had the group of men taken to jail. Not to leave anything out, I towed the cigar store owner's car just to add a little salt in the wound. Little did I know how deep the corruption was in Muncie, Indiana. The city I took an oath to serve and protect had a lot going on that a rookie cop did not comprehend, and this was a humiliating and rude awakening that I was not ready for. After all, at that time, I believed all police were honest and upstanding citizens.

A few minutes after we arrived back at the station, I was summoned to the chief's office. As I made my way to his office I was elated. I had done what others had not done. I was sure I would get a commendation for my good work. Boy, was I wrong. Instead of being congratulated for a job well done, I was reprimanded for not clearing the raid with the chief's office beforehand. I was confused. "Without the element of surprise it would not have been a successful raid, Chief," I explained.

The chief, who had recently taken over the office and had been appointed because of a change in politics, looked like a short, greasy-haired Mafia gangster. He was fuming and looked as if he would blow a blood vessel. ***"YOU DO NOT DO ANYTHING WITHOUT THE CHIEF KNOWING BEFOREHAND!"*** he shouted, pounding on his battered desk.

I had heard rumors of his dishonest ways, but being a green cop, I chose not to believe gossip. Besides, I believed that when you became an officer, you were to uphold the law, not break it.

Well, in a few weeks, they were back gambling, but at least I had brought some honor to the department instead of adding to the corruption that was going on in our "fair city."

A few days later, I was given a new assignment, chalking tires in the dead of winter. Chalking tires was the scud work of policing. For this assignment, you carried a large metal stick with a large piece of chalk on the end. It was my job to cover the entire town and chalk the tires of the cars parked on the streets. I would then return two hours later, and if the chalk mark was still in the same place, I would know that the car has been there over the two-hour parking limit, and I would then present the windshield with a ticket.

That winter was a killer with cold and deep snow week after week. Rumor had it that if I was not seen on the street chalking tires, I would be fired. I was too scared to even take a break or eat lunch. But sometimes I would sneak into a local hotel near the phone booth and empty my boots of snow. Many times I had frost bite and my feet were cracked and bleeding. But I was in the best shape I had ever been in and lost twenty pounds, which was great. However, I had lost so much more. I had lost the dream; the dream of honest cops and a clean city.

CHAPTER TWO

PRESSURE

O ne day, a veteran officer came to me and said he wanted to give me some information that I might find useful sometime. "Put this away for a time and DON'T tell anyone what I'm about to tell you," he warned. He walked me to a hallway in the back of City Hall and was acting as if he didn't want anyone to see us talking.

"No problem," I replied.

"I'm giving you this information to use when you need it, because it's not fair that they are trying to fire you or make you quit. The chief is a dog. Some of the officers think it is a disgrace to try and fire you. The chief is on the take. He has 'bag men' who go to the cigar stores and other places where they gamble to collect his take for letting them do their thing. Not only that, he has some officers on the night shift breaking into businesses. They break in, rob the businesses, split up the goods, then they call in the B&E and make out the reports. I know where they are storing the stuff that they steal. It's in one of the officers' garage."

I know my jaw dropped to the floor. I was in shock but became livid and wanted to raid the garage. However, the officer was adamant that I not do it.

"It would only end up in a shoot-out. These guys are playing for keeps. Right now, they are in the middle of planning a big heist. A captain is a part of the group, and they are to hit an armored car."

I didn't realize it at the time, but this information would save my rear end. I carried this information in my brain, not telling a soul about it. And it was haunting me day and night.

As I continued on my punishing assignment, it gave me the opportunity to completely observe our streets and what was happening on them. Walking the beat is the best source of information gathering. And as I chalked tires, I observed. I observed the "bag men" picking up the loot from payoffs from the gambling houses and prostitutes in the red light district. I vowed to fight even harder against the corrupt crap in my fine city.

Three or four weeks passed after I received the information, when, lo and behold, the chief summoned me to his office. "I am ready to accept your resignation now," he informed me.

I stood frozen in his office, but being five foot eight, I was taller than him and all of a sudden I got the boldness I needed. I said as loud as I could, "I'll make you a deal!!! You make your group of thieving cops that are committing B&Es in businesses and your best friend and captain who is planning the armored car heist resign and I will sign your papers."

He looked at me with great surprise and said nothing. Sweat appeared on his brow and his face turned white. He waved me out of the office. I didn't hear anything more about resignation for a little while. I noticed after that if I came face to face with him, he never made eye contact. That was fine with me. I just wanted the truth to be known, but sadly, my life as an officer would be over if I blew the whistle on him.

Soon after, the cop who gave me the information about the chief and his henchmen was caught carrying a TV out of a tent where it was being stored. A few months later, four of the officers I had been given the information about were arrested for the breaking and entering businesses. They were fired and had their day in court. It was front-page news in all the papers. Public opinion about the Muncie Police Department fell to an all-time low. I felt ashamed, and my morale was decreasing, along with a lot of other officers.

The media turned out to be what rescued me from my new assignment. A news reporter looked out his office window one day and watched as I struggled to chalk a tire that was covered with two feet of snow. He didn't like what he saw and wrote an editorial in the paper questioning whether "chalking tires was the best use of one of our female officers."

The resulting furor from the editorial helped put pressure on "the powers that be," and I was transferred to the Juvenile Aid Division. Wow! I had been brought in from the cold! But it was just the beginning of a campaign to have me quit, since I had become a threat to the front office. Guess no one ever rattled the cages before, since most of the other officers were content to just let things be as they were. I was brought in from the cold and that felt good to me. But the fat little chief was not through with me yet. Instead of giving me a respectable job, he assigned me to selling bike licenses in the Juvenile Office. What a bummer, but at least my feet were warm.

CHAPTER THREE
LIFE ON THE INSIDE

As one of the first police women in Muncie, along with my partner who was a college graduate, I had to prove myself over and over, and the stress level was tremendous. The end result was that I went into a deep depression, and my hair, which was always thick, started falling out. I would wake up in the mornings with large chunks of hair on my pillow. The divorce had taken a huge toll on me. It seemed no one could bring me out of the depression. My fellow officers carried the load for me as we worked in the field.

Working in the Juvenile Aid Division, some of the cases I was involved in were adding to the depression. Babies neglected, starving kids, children left alone to fend for themselves, battered children, children dead from gunshots, on and on. I would cry each night at the things I would see and have to investigate, but finally one day, I told myself, "You have to stop crying or quit the job." Quitting was not an option, so I stopped crying, but the hurt in my heart has never left me. I shall never forget some of the scenes of anguish and problems people have to face in their lives. It left a deep scar on my soul.

I worked in Juvenile Aid Division for seven years, long enough to learn to type statements, do interviews, interrogate, and solve crimes. It was the best training I could ever have for the day when I would become a detective sergeant. I had learned from the older investigators some of their tactics and took what I thought was the best of each. One JAD investigator fell in love with me. He was one of the greatest men I had ever known. Dark complexion with Italian roots, he was everything I would ever want in life. He was kind to me, loving and tender, but the thing was, he was married with four kids. That didn't sit well with everyone involved. Besides, that was when I met Mel, the man who would become my husband.

CHAPTER FOUR

MEL

Mel and I dated for two years before we got married. He was a teacher at the elementary school four blocks from my house that my daughter attended, and he had taken her under his wing. After a while, I began to wonder if he was coming to see me or was coming to the house to see my five-year-old daughter. He was so kind to her and to me. After a few years of marriage, however, things changed. Not with our daughter, but his attitude toward me.

If asked to describe Mel, I would have to say, "My husband is a wonderful person, but a terrible husband." He was quite selfish when it came to money. I was on my own when it came to that. Luckily, I had a good salary from the police department and later a nice pension. I lived on that, buying everything I needed, along with the children's clothes and household items, such as new furniture, a TV, etc. I was very good at saving and investing in stocks and bonds when the market was going well. Three years before I retired, I placed half of my salary into investments, and it paid off well.

Mel had been a bachelor for thirty-two years before we married and had always lived with his parents. After a few years of marriage, I would joke with him and tell him he should have stayed a bachelor. Although he is kind hearted as a person, his indifference toward me was heartbreaking at times, almost as devastating as if he had been violent. Maybe I deserved the indifference sometimes, but I had married to have a partner and companion; instead, though, I had a workaholic with nothing on his mind but work or recreation for himself.

My husband was a good man down deep, but even though I would not want to hurt him, I must say he was NEVER sensitive to my needs, leaving me alone every weekend as he attended a basketball game or coached or refereed a game.

Then there were the years when he bought a race car so he was gone every weekend for races. I learned to accept being alone as a big part of my married life. I tried very hard to get interested in his ball games and racing, but try as I may, it never clicked for me. I had to let him be involved in whatever made him happy and in the long run, the many years that we spent together ended up okay. As one of my friends would say, "It could be worse." Yes, it could be worse; at least I had a home and a father for my two girls, and for this I'm thankful. He didn't beat me like my first husband, and I don't regret the marriage; just wished it could have been more loving and that **some** of his interests had centered on me. Sounds selfish, but I know that is what every woman desires in a marriage.

As a teacher, Mel was loved by all his students and was voted Outstanding Teacher of the Year, something we were all proud of. Later in his life, he ran and was elected to the County Council, but that meant he was away from home even more than usual, what with meetings and political rallies. In fact, he was away from home most of our married life. I would joke to my friends that I wasn't sure that he knew I was gone when I was in Jamaica, but I was so very happy that he agreed to let me go.

Taking care of our 500 acres of farmland also kept him busy during the summer, and when we bought the new farm, which was called the Winchester Farm, it had a lovely dog and cat kennel. The White River ran through the land, and the motocross track was at the back of the property. The track ran over large hills, a small pond, and along the river.

After we took possession of the property, I wrote to the County Commissioners and asked them if they would consider backing me on creating an animal shelter, and since the county had none, I felt they might be interested. They came to the kennel, inspected it, and gave me a contract to start the first animal shelter in Randolph County. The kennel was located on the same property as the motocross track and was located about fifteen miles from our home . Then I hired caretakers to tend the kennel and the dogs and many casts and kittens that were brought in for us to care for. , Most day , I had to be present to advise and clean the animal pens. Loving animals as I do it was a good way to help find homes for these little creatures.

Talk about commitment and WORK ... the shelter had room for thirty dogs and fifteen cats, and we also began raising exotic animals. The exotic animals were at our farm where we lived. We had ostriches, emus, wolves, llamas, you name it we had them. It became one of the hardest jobs I have ever had. but one of the most enjoyable., they

We installed an eight foot nonclimbable fence, and the animals had over seven acres to graze. We were sponsored by three zoos in Indiana and, therefore, received their surplus animals either as gifts or by purchase at very low prices. We built small barns for some and the larger ones used our big barn. They all seemed to get along with each other except one day I saw one of our donkeys grab the neck of a llama. The llama sailed him through the air like a bullet. It was indeed a funny sight.

I loved being outdoors on the farm, even if the work was so very hard. I loved hearing the rooster crowing each morning, the donkeys braying, and the lion roaring. One of the gifts we received was a lion, and his roar could be heard over two miles away.

CHAPTER FIVE

LION IN THE CLOSET

Trigg, our lion, never knew he was a lion. He was just like a big kitten. He was ten days old, eyes still closed when we got him. When he opened his eyes, he saw us so he never knew he was a lion. He lived in the house with us and was housebroken and potty trained to use a large litter pan in the utility room. But as he grew, he would stand in the pan and his poop would fall out on the floor. He romped with my two daughters, running, hiding, playing tug-of-war with a towel or whatever he could find. He learned to walk on a leash and was invited to schools and parades. He would walk beside us like a trained dog; that is, until he became to weigh around 200 lbs and developed a mind of his own.

Mel, who was teaching sixth grade, started taking Trigg to school every day when we first got him, as he had to be fed his bottle three times during the day. It was very hard to find a "lion sitter" in those days. Trigg would ride in the front seat of the vehicle, causing a lot of drivers to do a double take and nearly crash when they would see Trigg hanging out of the window. The kids in Mel's class never missed a day of school because they were so excited to have a lion as a classmate. One boy who had missed over forty days of school the year before never missed a day again because he was the one who got to carry the lion from the car up to the classroom. Mel's classroom was on the third floor of the school, and Trigg had a security blanket that he lay on in the back of the room.

As the months went by and the school year was coming to a close, the principal told Mel that the lion was too big and could not come back to school. It broke the kids' heart, and they protested to Mel, so a plan was hatched so that Trigg could finish the school year. Mel would pull his vehicle to the back stairway, and they would sneak Trigg up the stairs, and no one would ever know. The school was very old with wooden floors, and they could hear if anyone approached the area.

One day they heard the principal, who, by the way, was an old military man and VERY strict, walking toward their room. The children grabbed the lion and his blanket and threw him into the coat closet, and luckily, the principal never knew he was there. Trigg got to finish the sixth grade, and we believe he is the only lion in the world that had a sixth-grade education.

At home he roamed the yard just like a dog would, peeing to mark his territory and staying within those boundaries. At times he would climb into one of our apple trees and sleep, sometimes causing old men driving by to swear off drinking. As he matured, he grew bigger and bigger and when he was ten months old we were forced to make a pen in the barn for him. He was so mad at us he refused to eat for over a week. He clearly did not enjoy being away from his family. We would let him out to romp with the dogs and to have his daily exercise, and he was always good about going back into his pen.

One day after putting the leash on him, he refused to go back into the barn. By then, he weighed about 400 lbs, so there was no tugging or pulling in the world that was going to make him move. We chained him to a tree near the barn that night, and Mel promised that he would try again in the morning. Believe me, I did not sleep well that night.

The next morning, Mel took him by the leash. I went behind with a metal wheelbarrow, and the sound that the wheelbarrow made was enough to scare him into the barn. This worked for months until one day as I was behind him with the wheelbarrow, he stopped, sat down facing the wheelbarrow, and took his very large paw and hit it with a crashing blow. I knew then he would have to be forever caged in the barn.

He was relativity happy in the barn, playing with his bowling ball, knocking it from pillar to post, eating his meals, and playing with us through the bars. He lived until he was fifteen years old, the maximum age most lions live in captivity. It was a sad day when he quit eating and lay down to die. He had been so much a part of our family, lovable, playful, and, oh, so sweet, as he would jump in my lap and suck my thumb, closing his eyes and going to sleep in my arms.

CHAPTER SIX

SAVED IN THE '70S

I was reassigned to the Public Relations Division for a year, and although it was not my cup of tea, I tried to make the best of it. Back in uniform and usually behind a desk, I really started dreading going to work. I was happy, however, that it was the day shift and I could still be at home with the family in the evenings. Later that year, I was reassigned to the Juvenile Division.

I began having pain in the right side of my face and neck. Then it moved upward to the right side of my head. At first, I attributed the pain to stress, but as the days went by and the pain intensified, I became worried and finally consulted my doctor. He found a small nodule in the side of my right cheek. By then, the pain was so excruciating that I could hardly function. His prognosis was shocking. He said it could be cancer and that I might lose the nerves in the side of my face, leaving me with a sagging face on one side. He scheduled surgery immediately.

I went home in a daze and called Elaine, my friend of twenty-five years who was a nurse. She came over immediately and told me that she was going to take me to a church service on Wednesday night. She said she had heard of healings that were taking place at the little church. I really didn't want to go but she insisted.

"Okay, what can it hurt? I am in so much pain I am willing to try anything," I told her.

When Wednesday came, she drove and we made our way to the little church in the countryside.

When I entered the church, I immediately sensed that something momentous would happen. I felt a presence that I had never felt before. We took a seat near the front of the church and joined in heartily in the singing and praying. During the service, the elders called me to the front of the church. Elaine and I were surprised since we were visitors to the church and didn't expect that anyone there would know us.

The minister and some of the elders stood around me, placing their hands on my head and shoulders. They began praying, and some were speaking in a language that I did not recognize. It was scary at first, but then I decided to relax and be in the moment. All of a sudden, I felt like I was floating and being lifted off the floor. It was the weirdest feeling I have ever experienced. The strangest thing of all was the fact that I was pain free for the first time after six weeks of agony. When I put my hand on the nodule, it was still there, but there was no pain. All the way home I kept telling Elaine, "The pain is gone, the pain is gone."

When I reached home, I ran into my living room, grabbed Mel, and swung him around the room, jumping and squealing with joy, still yelling, "The pain is gone." I had another appointment with the doctor before the surgery which was scheduled for two days later. After examining me again, he was puzzled. "Maybe we should wait on the surgery for a while," he said. "I believe the growth is dissipating." A few more weeks and the nodule had completely disappeared.

I began attending the little church in the country and was amazed at the teachings and beliefs. It was a Full Gospel church, and they believed literally everything in the Bible. Well, that was good enough for me. After all, I had received a healing from God, and now I was on fire for what He can do and what He had done. I started telling everyone who would listen, and even those who didn't, about the healing I had experienced, and it wasn't long before other fellow police officers began attending the church. When you have experienced God's work and love and mercy personally, it is the best and most wonderful way to explain the gospel to people.

The charismatic Christian movement was going strong in our area in the early '70s, and many people who had become stale in their churches were turning to churches that believed in modern-day miracles and the movement of the Holy Spirit. It was an exciting time to attend church. It was an exciting time to become "saved." It certainly turned my life around and many others that I knew.

The testimonies of people who had experienced healings and miracles were mind-boggling, and the Holy Spirit was blowing over the country like a whirlwind, with Full Gospel churches growing like crazy. It was a time filled with love for our fellow man and a time to see many come to the Lord. Although I always knew there was a God, now I was able to know Him with passion and realize that He works in my life every day. I knew from that day that I wanted to be in His perfect will at all times.

CHAPTER SEVEN

NEW ASSIGNMENT

I was still working in the Juvenile Division when there were rumors that a merit commission was being formed. The merit system was established in the mid-'60s, and each officer had to be tested. This was a rough time for most of the officers, but I was able to pass the test for sergeant and was excited to think "maybe" things could be fair when it came to the operation of the department. I was elevated to juvenile investigator through the Merit Board exams. The good ole' boys club was over and the spoils system was thrown out the window.

Our police department worked under the old system of political patronage. When the political representatives changed, there would be a big shake-up in the police and fire departments. This was what the old system did, the old machine of politics; the unfair and care-not system. But in every dark cloud there is a silver lining. In the mid-'70s, a new mayor was elected, and the fat little Mafia-looking chief was finished. Hallelujah!!! This time, the system was working for me.

Over the years, I had stayed as far away as possible from joining either side of the political arena. I felt safe that way, but being new to how the system worked in Muncie, I had made a fatal mistake. New assignments were always given when a new chief takes over. Your shift assignment was directed by what party you were loyal to; your promotions were decided by how you had voted throughout the years, and if you had worked in the open for a party or political hopeful, you could end up being a captain or sergeant. That is how the "old spoil" system worked. It all changed some years later when a merit commission was established.

Under the new regime, my brother left the sheriff's department and joined the Muncie Police Department. He quickly rose to the position of deputy chief and built respect among the officers. He was a fine boss to the men, and everyone liked him.

He had always been a good officer, but for reasons unknown to everyone, he was demoted to patrolman. Then he seemed to lose interest in the job of a policeman. I don't know, but I always felt he had been disappointed, disillusioned, and broken from trying to find justice in the corrupt system. I was sure it was on a much larger scale than I would ever know. He never told me and hasn't to this day. In my eyes, he was still my hero and always would be. Nothing could change that.

He lives with his wife of many years who by the way was a model wife and one that I wished I could be more like. They raised three boys who made our family proud. Although his life as it dipped to a low, rebounded quickly and honorably.

What I didn't realize at that time was that alcoholism was a disease that ran in my family on both sides. As a child growing up, drinking seemed a way of life with aunts, uncles, cousins, and all of my parents' friends. Drinking and being drunk out of their heads was normal. Of my mother's eight sisters and brothers, only three did not abuse alcohol. So at all our family reunions, beer and hard drinks would flow. Their drinking and obnoxious behavior repulsed me, and as a child, I told myself that I would never drink. I'm sure this was God's way of saving me from becoming an alcoholic. I do not believe in generational curses but do believe we are born with traits that are weaknesses for certain things. Drinking alcohol has been proven to me that our family carries this weakened gene.

With the regime change and new bosses, I swallowed my pride and begged for a transfer to the Detective Division. I had been a juvenile investigator for seven years, and seeing battered kids, neglected children, and crimes committed by juveniles, I was ready for a change.

CHAPTER EIGHT
NEW DAY

On the last day for assignment changes, I was ordered to the new chief's office. "The order has come down. You are to be transferred to the Detective Division," he informed me. I was walking on air as I shook his offered hand.

"Chief, you'll never be sorry for transferring me. I will work as hard as I can." And I did. I threw myself into the work, putting in lots of overtime as I began cultivating informants. I worked extra long hours and took each case very seriously, solving most of them.

Soon the work began paying off, and I began solving cases. But my captain didn't like the idea of having a woman in the Detective Division, so he made life as miserable as possible for me, giving me cases that were petty, oftentimes assigning me a case that I would have to go out on just at quitting time. Capt. Jackson was a loudmouth and intimidating. He walked around like a caveman; the only thing he didn't do was beat on his chest.

One day a call came in just a few minutes before time to leave for the day. The captain walked by four detectives and came to the back office where I had my desk and gave me the call. He was so arrogant and loud, puffing on his cigar. He handed me the paper with the address of the call. The afternoon shift could have taken the call. It was just a petty crime that could have waited an hour or so for the new shift.

It was quitting time, and I'm sure the "boys" had a golf game to get to. Well, I wasn't having any of it. I jumped up from my seat and left via the back door, refusing to accept the paper with the address of the call that he was trying to hand me. I was so fed up and tired of this type of treatment which had been going on for months. The big cigar-smoking captain had picked on me for the last time.

As I crossed the street to go to the parking lot, I glanced behind and saw that he was running after me. I jumped in my car, and he stood in front of the car to block me. I gunned the engine and started off. He had to jump to the side to avoid being hit, and as I passed him I yelled, "See you in the chief's office tomorrow morning. Discrimination is not going to be tolerated." That was the last time he messed with me, knowing I would stand up for myself and that I could be someone to reckon with.

In the Detective Division, I had several different partners, learning from each of them. Each one had his own way of interviewing suspects and investigating crimes, and I would gleam the best out of each. My expertise became a method of having the suspects confess to me. I don't know if it was the "mother's touch" or the soft voice after the harsh voices of those male detectives, but I had a way of getting confessions when no one else could. Many a hardened criminal would confess some hideous crime to me, and the case would be solved. I began getting calls in the middle of the night from my fellow detectives who needed my assistance in interrogating a suspect

My reputation was gaining momentum on the street as well as with my comrades. One afternoon as I was typing my last case report, trying to quickly finish and get home at a decent hour, a young, uniformed officer entered my office. This uniformed officer seemed nervous as he stood there. "I have some good information," he stammered without giving any details.

It was not unusual for street cops to give information that they had gathered on the street to detectives. I tried to put him at ease, but it didn't seem to help much.

"Look, Patrolman, I'm tired and want to go home. Spit it out or come back when you feel you can trust me. Oh, by the way, why did you decide to give me the info when there are fourteen other detectives in the division?" I asked.

Looking at the floor he replied, "Your reputation on the street is that you are honest and beat a case to death."

This response took me off guard, but nevertheless made me proud. I immediately softened my approach with him. "Sorry, I didn't get your name, Patrolman," I smiled.

"My name is Phil, but they call me Popeye," he responded, this time looking me in the eye.

This was the first time I met Popeye, and the first time he brought me information. There would be many such times in the days to follow.

CHAPTER NINE
DETECTIVE SERGEANT SURPREME

Popeye kept the fire going with information. He had apparently cultivated some good confidential informants and was hustling up great leads on a rash of robberies that had broken out in Muncie. Our investigations revealed that the gang of thieves was burglarizing homes, fencing the stolen stuff, and outrunning the police each time. The thieves would also break into gun shops and clean them out. The ring was excellent at what they did, and the fencing operation involved trading the guns to Cuba for drugs.

Sometimes you receive information that is reliable, but the informant is not willing to help act on the case. Then you find the case dead in the water. Good informants will work by your side until the case ends in an arrest and recovered property.

But with the information coming in from Popeye's sources, we managed to detain a suspect for questioning. He was good at what he did and as slippery as they come, but we managed to bring him in. When we confronted him about his part in the fencing of thousands of dollars of stolen goods, he was cocky and full of contempt when he told us "You are beating your heads against the wall because so many big shots are involved in the receiving of the expensive goods that no one is going to be prosecuted to any extent."

Steve was one we felt could blow the whistle on some of the big players in the corruption ring. He was also in tight with a wrecker service that was fencing the guns and stolen cars. Steve was tall, lanky, and could run like a fox. He was good at his game, a true punk that could outthink the cops.

"I scope out the vehicles until the wrecker service arrives, hook on to the cars, and take them to the wrecker yard and strip them," he told me once. Of course, he did not give me any details, just enough information to make my mouth water. He was one criminal I wanted to nail against the wall, but to tell the truth, he was always one step ahead of us.

The wrecking service and yard was co-owned by a Muncie deputy sheriff. It was all a big ball of criminals and officials bound together so tightly and the roots were so deep that we were going to have a hard time penetrating their game. But that didn't stop us from raiding the various premises that we were told about by the suspect and recovering over a million dollars of stolen goods, including riding lawn mowers, jewelry, antiques, and appliances.

We did not get to the bottom of the gun running because when it was brought up, every suspect lost it. It was a subject no one in Muncie, Indiana, wanted to talk about. One suspect, an older man by the name of Whitey, started shaking all over and began crying. "I can't talk about that. There are big officials involved in this part of the operation, right up the ladder to officials in high places," he told us. We had touched a raw nerve when it came to the guns.

Some years later, we determined that the guns were being shipped to the Contras in Central America, a network that some small-time officers in Muncie, Indiana, were not going to stop. What a network they must have had. Years of stealing guns, then moving them to another country and then receiving money or contraband for their trouble. This was a heavily guarded network, one that had been in place for a few years.

With the hard work by Popeye and cases being solved with the information he provided, the chief took notice and assigned Popeye to work full time with me. This was an unprecedented move, assigning a uniformed officer into the detective division, but we were happy that he was given the chance to work exclusively with me. Of course, the skeptics could be heard asking, "Man, what can a patrolman and a female detective do?"

All we needed was a little time to show them. Popeye was as determined as I was to stop the flow of criminal activities.

CHAPTER TEN

POPEYE AND WAYNE

M̲y newly assigned partner, Popeye, was honest and hard to understand, but we worked well together and had the same goals:
arresting the bad guys and putting them away for a long time. Popeye
would become my closest friend; sometimes a worrywart, but he always had my back and kept me motivated. He was one of the hardest
working cops I had ever come across in my career. He wanted the
cases solved, and he wanted it yesterday. No fooling around; just find
out who did what and get them off the street.

Popeye got his name from his large cheeks. His dark hair had begun to recede. It seemed he was always huffing and puffing when he
was close to a lead that would solve a case. I began to realize his habits,
and after a couple of months working with him, I was able to tell what
was going on before he even spoke about it. He was an easy read for
me, and maybe that is why we worked so well together. He kept his
word when he told you he would and loved to kid around but was dead
serious when it came to work.

Later that year, I was assigned a new partner, Wayne. He was a
seasoned detective with a few years under his belt. I would work cases
with Wayne when Popeye had days off.

Wayne was tall, blond, well built, and very good looking. He had a
lot of women chasing him and calling him all the time. He was a well-
defined detective with great interviewing skills. I was happy to have
him as a partner because I was learning much about his methods of
interviewing suspects. It was a learn-learn situation, a time to watch
and pick up some traits that I could use later on in my investigative
years that lay ahead.

Wayne had been assigned a murder case before we were partners. He obsessed every day over the case even though he was ordered to close the file since the case had gone cold. He had spent hours and hours putting together the case, but it was turned down by the prosecutor, making everyone wonder why.

The prosecutor, Markel, had been a top-notch lawyer, known to "twist" a case, and had friends he could call on in order to win a case. He had never been known to be an honest lawyer, but as a prosecutor, he was living in a fish bowl. That didn't seem to matter to him, though. He was always finding a way to "twist" a case.

Wayne knew it was a good case and one that could bring a conviction. When he would start talking about the case, which was every day, I started to understand his conviction and his passion about the death of this young mother. I believe the case was on his mind all the time, and as the months passed, it also became my passion to see the dirty SOB who killed the young mother hang for the murder. It was a solid case, one that could be prosecuted and the suspect convicted, but for some strange reason, in Muncie, Indiana, Delaware County, there was a foul odor in the air.

The case involved the murder of a young mother who was beaten to death in front of her five-year-old son, Eric, who was also beaten and left for dead. The battered little boy, who had witnessed the murder before being beaten, was rushed to the intensive care unit at the hospital in Indianapolis, and police officers, when allowed to question the boy, were told by the prosecutor not to mention the details to him; only let him bring up what he remembered. Well, that sounded okay, as we knew an investigator or police person can not put ideas into the victim's or suspect's psyche. All the details must come from them.

The facts were that the young mother was five feet tall, weighed 100 pounds, while the suspect, her boyfriend, was six foot three and weighed 250 pounds. She had been trying to break up with him. Her boyfriend had a history of beating her, one time running her car off the road, and reaching through the window and slamming her head into the steering wheel. Witnesses placed him at the scene at the time of the murder, and a neighbor in the other side of the duplex heard a female voice saying, "What the hell are you doing?" It was determined by an autopsy that she died of massive trauma to the head from a blunt object.

The boyfriend was given not one but two polygraph tests, and flunked them both. But then, a questionable third polygraph was arranged by the prosecutor's office. He was taken to Chicago for the third polygraph test and escaped from the police in Chicago after the test was run. Why in the world would he run if he thought he was going to pass the test? It was street knowledge that the lie detector test in Chicago was a farce, a tool to have reason to release him. We were all sure that someone in Chicago owed a favor to the illustrious prosecutor. The boyfriend turned himself in only when he was told that he had passed that test.

Word circulating on the street was that he was going to blow the whistle on a bunch of big shots if he was charged. It became very clear that he had information on some officials because the case was then closed by the prosecutor's office, even though it had been proven by witnesses, polygraphs, and a thorough investigation. What in the hell was going on in our fair justice system? Was it really this corrupt?

Eric grew into a young man. One day he called me and with desperation in his voice asked me if there was anything that was being done to bring this monster to justice. He said he remembered the beatings and could always identify the person who did the murder. His call affected me greatly. Here was a young man, growing up without his mother, remembering the murder and crying out to find out WHY the man that did this gruesome murder was not behind bars. I was forced to tell him that the corruption in our city was so deep that when someone has information on the judges, prosecutors, or lawyers it was impossible to get a case prosecuted. We could see it happening

daily in front of our eyes. In some cases, when suspects were arrested for anything, they had the prosecutor's office, dirty lawyers, and
judges that would look the other way for a sum of money. How can
you explain to a young man who has missed growing up with a doting
mother, missing all their Christmases together, birthdays, graduation,
and other special times, that he lives in a city where murder doesn't
matter??

This case started to get to me and I became as obsessed as my
partner. I often wondered how I would feel if we ever got the chance
to interrogate the SOB that beat his girlfriend to death. At this point
in my career, I wanted nothing else but to see him rot in jail. I thought
about it all the time. How could our city be so corrupt that a murderer
could walk the streets a free man?

I became totally consumed by the thought of putting the SOB away
forever. Seems to me it was an open-and-shut case, a victory for all
who had worked so many hours on the case, but in Muncie, Indiana,
there was a rotten smell in the air. This case would haunt me, and as
a result, I dove into the biggest bunch of white-collar criminals our
county had ever seen, let alone known about. They had been as slick
as the justice system could hide. Each unit of the government was
penetrated. They could call on each other anytime, night or day, and
"things" would be taken care of. We were sure that it was as thick as
the national Mafia but on a local level. They knew things about each
other, could pay high prices for silence, paid off judges, and would kill
or bomb cars if nothing else worked. These guys played for keeps. This
was not a laughing matter.

CHAPTER ELEVEN

BROTHERS IN BLUE

O ur success rate with cases soon became an embarrassment of riches as fellow detectives began asking Popeye and me to slow down with the cases solved as we were beginning to make them look bad. We were solving 30 to 50 cases each month, and these statistics were sent to the front office each month. Although I know the men in the division were proud of me and excited about the recovery of property, they gave me a hard time anyway. It was just their way of showing me they approved. But not all cases brought glory.

One day, an informant came to the station to tell me that there was a lady in Shed Town who was performing illegal abortions and burying the fetus in her backyard. Shed Town was a slum that consisted of blocks of small run-down houses or shanties with large families living in them. These were "hillbillies" who came to Indiana from the South to earn a living. They stuck together like glue and never gave any information to anyone. If a woman from the area was reporting to the police, there must be some validity to the claim. Police never went to Shed Town to get information from anyone since they would never tell on each other.

After I questioned the informant, I was convinced. She signed a statement swearing that her information was true, and we began an investigation. Our chief really got excited over the information and decided to send a backhoe to the yard to start digging. This was big news for the *Muncie Star and Press* and each move we made was reported in detail. I objected to the chief's course of action, telling the chief that a backhoe was too big for the job; that it should be dug like an archaeology dig. But I was ignored. The media attention had the department heads and some of the cops hamming it up.

After the entire backyard was nothing but piles of dirt and nothing was found, the chief agreed that maybe we should have been more careful. Nothing was ever found, and the informant that gave us the information ended up murdered in Ohio. We had made a boo-boo with the investigation and ended up with egg on our face, but we were shaking the bushes and that was all that counted. When we got information, we would check it out. If it checked out, we went after the case like roaring lions, beating every lead to death.

Once, when we had one suspect in handcuffs, the slippery one that had a friendship with the prosecutor, Steve, a suspect that we had tried to arrest for months, as he was finally being led away in shackles from my office, he turned and said, "You are one persistent bitch. You never give up. You beat a case to death." That was the greatest compliment I ever had from a criminal.

I can't remember a criminal that I couldn't find something to like about his or her personality. No, I didn't like their crimes, but after you spend time with them, interrogating them, taking statements of confession, you learn a lot about their psyche. You learn that they are just human beings that have made bad choices and maybe not have had any support growing up.

I had some great friends in the department; the ones I was close with were all hardworking and honest. I prided myself on their work, and they were with me to the end of my career. Two such officers, Larry and Linda, fell in love and were married in my backyard. We had so much enjoyment picking out flowers, decorating the gazebo, getting all the plans together. They were such a beautiful couple and so much in love. The wedding was in the late afternoon with the sunshine just right for photographs. It was a day to remember and is etched in my memory as if it happened yesterday.

Larry was one of the few who worked for me when I was in the chief's office that I trusted. He worked in the Intelligence Division and was in his late 30s when he came to my office one day and complained of a pain in his left arm. I advised him to see a doctor, but as cops, we always think we are invincible, tough, young, and active; no real reason to go to a doctor. Larry died a short time later after of a massive heart attack. Linda, his wife of thirteen years, still grieves his death. She finished her tour of duty on the department and since retirement, lives quietly by herself.

I feel privileged to have worked with great officers, learning their ways of staying cool in the face of danger, keeping their sanity when it seemed the whole world had gone crazy, and still keeping a sense of humor. It was great knowing the men and women in blue that were honest and wanted to protect and serve.

Out of a department of 122 men and women, I felt a bond with all of them. I had no doubt that each would back me up if need be, and I knew I would do the same for them. I remember when I was a rookie I called out at an address and gave a signal seven. What I meant to say was ten = seven, but not knowing my signals well enough, I had just radioed the signal for extreme danger, like an officer shot or something worse. I was amazed to turn around on the porch of the house to see four police cars rolling up to help.

When they realized the situation, they explained to me with a big laugh the mistake I had made. Often, when you join the force, you are so naïve, so green, and ready to save the world. Soon after you get a very large wake up call that your days in the blue uniform are hampered by politics or corruption or both.

You are quickly disillusioned, but you have to make a conscious decision to be either an honest and hardworking cop, or you become lazy, telling yourself it's not worth it. A lot of officers just put in their eight hours and walk away from it after twenty years with a nice pension, or they become involved with the work and the people they serve and walk away, proud to have been a part of the history of the Muncie Police Department.

I, for one, along with my small army of officers, ranked as the proud and hardworking ones. We really didn't care that we were some-times the brunt of jokes or that there was jealousy within the ranks. We kept focused on what was hurting the population, their children, and the reputation of the department. We could hold our heads high and honor the badge and the trust that is given with it.

CHAPTER TWELVE

NEW PLAYERS IN TOWN

As the seventies came to a close, the impact of the economic down-turn was felt hard in America. More than a hundred thousand jobs had disappeared, with a lot of factories closing or moving their operations overseas where labor was cheaper. Illegal drugs were hitting our nation hard, and I was on fire to keep my city clean and letting all the drug lords know me by my reputation. But my team started noticing that there was a new kind of criminal and drug dealer operating in Muncie.

We started seeing a proliferation of gangs operating in the Midwest and hearing gang names that we had never heard before. Further investigation revealed that a gang based in the eastern states of America called the Gangster Disciples had joined forces with a Jamaican outfit known as the Shower Posse to control the importation and distribution of marijuana and cocaine. The Gangster Disciples, starting in the early '70s, had cashed in on America's craving for drugs, running the cocaine trade from the U.S. ports where the drugs were shipped in from Colombia, and then transported by car to the Midwest. Gangster Disciples and the Shower Posse had similar operating styles, and they were unlike any other gangs we had encountered.

Their business operation was structured like a Fortune 500 company, with a chairman and board of directors, managers, and workers. Operations were funded and fueled by the proceeds of drug running and drug dealing. The Gangster Disciples, or GD, as they preferred to be called, dressed in suits, carried briefcases, and rivaled the Mafia in wealth and power. They laundered their money by the suitcase full in the Cayman Islands and Panama.

Jamaica had always been the Mecca of ganja (marijuana) growing, and now, through Kingston Wharves, the largest port in the Caribbean, had become a major transhipment point for the cocaine coming into the U.S. from South America. The drug trade was controlled by the Shower Posse, who were affiliated in Jamaica with the Jamaica Labor Party (JLP) and who controlled the port and the adjoining communities of Tivoli Gardens and West Kingston. A portion of the drug shipments going into Jamaica was used to buy guns and to finance corrupt politicians, policemen, and gang activities.

Shower Posse members were ruthless with total disregard for human life and had gained a fierce reputation in the United States for brutality as they would "shower" their targets with bullets. Their Posse members oftentimes acted as hit men for the New York Italian Mafia, and unlike other gangs, did not hesitate to kill police officers. In their collaboration with the Gangster Disciples, they supplied the middle managers, muscle, and enforcers for the Gangster Disciples. Local Muncie kids were the street dealers. I would take a hard view on these guys and vowed to give them as hard a time as I could. And that I did.

In January of 1980, a new mayor was elected, and he was interviewing officers in the department for appointments to the front office. He was going to appoint a new chief and three deputies. We heard rumor after rumor about who they would be, and my name came up a couple of times. I was not sure of the rumor until one afternoon the new mayor knocked on my front door. He sat with my husband and me and talked of what he wanted to see happen in the next four years. He was honest and had idealistic ideas of how the city should be led. He then asked me if I would consider being chief of investigations.

"Only if no one in the city is off limits. And you allow my team to have complete autonomy," I answered.

"If they are breaking the law, you will not be pulled off any case," he replied.

I was delighted at his answer. I knew that I had a handful of officers that I could trust and I knew right away who I would want to be my backups and confidants. They were like my brothers, always backing me up, making sure that I was safe in our fight against crime.

CHAPTER THIRTEEN
TRACKING THE CARTEL

Just as I became chief of investigations, a female informant gave us a tip that a deputy prosecutor who co-owned a plane with a deputy sheriff had flown in a large amount of marijuana from Florida. "I was on the flight with him. This was his private plane," she told us. "You can check it out. It's a Cherokee with a number on the tail N32762," she added.

Oh my God. Now, finally, this was the break we had needed so badly.

Further investigation by my office confirmed that the deputy prosecutor and deputy sheriff both had pilots' licenses and were co-owners of a Cherokee with the same N number. Things were beginning to make sense, the fact that it was next to impossible to get a drug case prosecuted in our county. I knew I had to find a way to bust the big guys in order to stop some of the traffic. I was totally prepared for the fact that it would not be easy and that we would only put a small dent into the drug trade, but at the same time, I was excited that we had the break that we had needed for months. This information had to be protected and was classified.

I had a handful of men I could trust, one being my friend and confidant, Popeye. He had been there through thick and thin and was always in my corner with advice and backup. He wanted to see the big guys behind bars as badly as I did. We had great hopes and dreams of taking down these dirty officials.

Our new mayor, true to his word when he asked me to become chief of investigations, was behind the idea of going after the corrupt officials but still had to keep his job security and relationship with the courthouse crew. The mayor was a former lawyer, really green as they come, and didn't know much about the running of the police department. We would have meeting after meeting with him, trying to explain the workings of the department, but to this day, I'm not sure he got the picture. Although he gave me carte blanche about getting the "bad guys," I am not sure he knew the ramifications of the outcome. Perhaps we did not know either. He had come up out of the ranks with these guys, therefore, would, someday, have to work back in their courtrooms and offices.

With the information we gathered, we began working with the local FBI agent. Ray had been transferred to the Muncie office a couple of years earlier. Ray was a short, bald, 50-something who walked as if he were ten feet tall. He seemed interested in our investigation, and it wasn't long before we started including him in our circle. We asked him for advice, but it seemed he never really had an answer for us. We began wondering why the feds were not doing anything with the information we were able to supply to Ray. We trusted him, worked with him, and then, to our utter disappointment, we learned he was as bad as, or worse, than the ones we were trying to put in jail. We put so much faith in the agent, only to learn that he was as crooked as a dog's hind leg. He drank heavily and would tip off the prosecutor's office to classified information on our cases. He was later forced to resign from the FBI, and we then learned that nothing we had turned over to him had been filed with the head office in Indianapolis. Betrayal, it seemed, was everywhere.

We took some of our information to the state police. This was classified information of an ongoing investigation into large pieces of farm equipment that was being stolen and taken to Kentucky to a farm belonging to a deputy sheriff and his brothers who owned a wrecker service and wrecking yard in Muncie. This was the same deputy that owned the airplane and was being protected by the prosecutor. A prominent Muncie lawyer was also implicated, so it was crucial for the investigation to be kept top-drawer classified.

In our meeting with the state police, we emphasized the importance of the information, asking them to **PLEASE** keep it confidential because not only was it classified information, but without the authorization of the chief to travel to the state police, our jobs would be on the line. When we returned to the Muncie Department later that evening, we were surprised to find a note on the chief's door. It was a note from the radio room informing the chief that we had been in Indianapolis talking to the state police. We had been doubled-crossed by the state police investigator too. We cringed as we had not received permission to go and we knew the chief would be irate with us for not informing him. A chewing out was what we received, and we were thankful for that. He could have suspended us.

Our chief of police, Gene, was as honest as they came, and being a Christian, was a great attribute to the office of chief. I believe this was a first for the department as some of our previous chiefs were very corrupt. Gene was loved and respected by all who knew him, and when he told you something, you knew it to be the truth. I remember that when he took office, he made it policy that at Christmas we turn down the hams and turkeys offered by the wrecker service because he did not want us to be indebted to anyone. I was proud to work with him and for him. He was truly a man of honor and one who replaced all the negatives that other chiefs had left behind.

But despite the chief being one of the most honest cops I had ever known, we chose not to keep him informed of what we were into Need to know basis we told each other.. Because we didn't know the Indians from the cowboys, we kept things on a need-to-know basis, which seemed to be okay with him, although he was not fully aware of what we knew. At that point in our investigation and after being betrayed by the FBI, we didn't trust anyone.

I always believed the chief was honest, but some of the company he was associated with was a little shaky, and human nature can sometimes cause us to talk too much. One of the other deputy chiefs who was in charge of the uniform division had two sides of his mouth going at the same time. This was a known factor by anyone who was close to him. His privy to what went on in the chief's office was a deep concern to our investigative team. He relished in being in the "know," and then reporting it to whoever would gain him prominence. It must have made him feel important to be able to relay information to others. We had to watch what we said in front of him.

Soon it became a volatile situation for me and my fellow officers who were working the cases. Our lives and families were on the line, not to mention our jobs. Pressure from all sides seemed to always be at our door. We were dealing with the "big boys." Looking over our shoulders all the time, not trusting anyone, now including the state police investigator, the FBI agent who was tipping our hand to the prosecutor's office, I slept with two guns beside my bed and one under my pillow. That is when I started wearing an ankle holster with a small 38 along with my Smith and Wesson in my purse. Mace, a slapper, handcuffs and I.D. made my purse heavy on my right shoulder.

CHAPTER FOURTEEN
THE BUST

As our investigations continued, we made friends with a customs officer who called me one day stating that a known drug smuggler was flying in and out of the Muncie airport. He didn't have much information about the plane, but knew the N number on the tail. I stationed an officer at the airport when I got a tip that a private Cherokee airplane was going to take off from a neighboring city.

Now, the fact is, we knew that a deputy sheriff was co-owner of an airplane along, with the deputy prosecutor, and it had a certain N number on the tail. We figured that the plane our contact in customs had tipped us about might be the plane the deputy sheriff had flown with a load of marijuana into Delaware County from Florida. This could possibly be the same information that our female informant had given us. Turns out this plane was owned by one of the largest drug smugglers in the Midwest and was headed for Jamaica to pick up ganja. The plane had two large fuel tanks, and the seats had been removed. It looked as if they were going for the mother lode.

While I put things in motion to get a warrant to detain the plane, Popeye and another intelligence officer drove to the airport, getting into a position where they could photograph the plane. My contact in customs was on the phone to me giving me updated information which I would then relay to the two at the airport. Well, lo and behold, much to everyone's surprise, the deputy sheriff we had been investigating showed up with a large black bag and boarded the plane with the known drug smuggler.

Popeye called all excited. "I have the airplane in view, and if we don't hurry, we will lose the plane as it looks as if they are about to take off."With sirens blaring and backup officers, I drove my unmarked car to the airport and straight unto the tarmac. To our disappointment, we didn't have the correct plane; the N number on the plane was one number different than the number we had from our informant. Therefore, our warrant was invalid. The plane took off. I stood beside the squad car watching as the plane flew above a cloud and vanished. I can't remember when I had ever been so disappointed and felt as if the months of investigation had been in vain.

After the hullabaloo calmed down, I was summoned into the office of the bigwigs at the airport who told me it was against the law to drive unto the tarmac. Four men in suit and ties stared at me as if I had two heads. They were all very upset with me, and truth be known, I shut my ears to their redbrick. Then I returned fire. ***"MY MEN WILL GO ANYWHERE IN ORDER TO STOP THE DRUG TRAFFIC,"*** I shouted and demanded that air traffic control and customs track the plane that had taken off.

"You're wasting my time with this, I have a load of drugs to track."

The locals managed to locate it on radar, but lost it somewhere in Kentucky. We later learned that the plane went down in the Florida Everglades.

Not fazed, my team continued its investigation. Our intelligence information and investigation became the start of a very large-scale operation, and the outcome was many meetings conducted with and by the FBI offices in Fort Wayne, South Bend, and Detroit. Finally, the feds were taking our investigations seriously.

In our investigation, all leads were centered on the deputy sheriff and his cohorts, which, in turn, led into the larger probe ending up in Michigan. Our investigation led to the arrest of nine subjects, including Dennis Sobczak, also known as Peter Andresean, who distributed more than 80,000 pounds of marijuana with a street value of more than $50 million. He was indicted on ten counts of perjury in Michigan for testimony he gave to the Grand Jury about the smuggling operations and sentenced to four years in prison. A few months later, the feds seized a golf course in Michigan where some of the money had been laundered.

This was not child's play. It was big-time, uptown stuff. These were the big boys of the smuggling trade, at least in the Midwest. We would have netted more in the Muncie Mafia if the FBI agent who had sold us out had kept his mouth shut. We were proud and happy with the results, however, and felt that our little band of officers agents had done well.

CHAPTER FIFTEEN
CONSEQUENCES

While my team was proud of our successes, this only threw fuel on the fire. The prosecutor's office was now after us big time. Now they HAD to stop us at any cost. If we were to reveal and expose them for what they were involved in, their lives, jobs, and reputations would be ruined. I began receiving verbal threats by phone that if I didn't back off, all my rare and exotic animals on the farm would end up dead. Anyone that knew me was well aware that the animals were a very large part of my life and that I loved them a lot. They were playing mind games, but I was not going to stop the investigation; in fact, it made me more determined to push ahead. We had a sweep of our personal phones and found that they were being tapped.

A policeman had gotten close to some information and later had his car bombed. He lived, but the experience shook us all to the core. With the death threats and the memory of the car bombing, our little band of men had plenty of worries. I know I'm hardheaded at times, and what they were doing to make us stop only made me work harder to get to the bottom of the Muncie Cartel.

Then, early one morning, Popeye and his wife were leaving their home when a shot rang out, hitting the passenger side of the vehicle. It was a close call. Three days later, one of our best informants called to say a hit man had been brought into town to kill both me and Popeye. According to the information which he had overheard at the local wrecker service owned by the deputy's brother, the "hit man" had been given only a small amount of cash for the job and later chickened out when he learned we were cops. The information was the hit man was going to be paid $400. We had a good laugh to think that our lives were not worth more that $400 but still knew they were playing for keeps.

Most of our energy became directed at making sure none of us was gunned down or harmed. Popeye and I would put Scotch tape or small pebbles on the hoods of our cars at night. In the morning if the tape was broken, we knew that someone had tampered with the vehicle. Sometimes our imagination would run wild and we would be driving along and think we smelled gunpowder. We would stop, jump out of the car, and search it until we were satisfied that all was okay. We began to get very paranoid, and I'm sure some of the other officers thought we were acting very strange. What they didn't realize was we could not trust anyone, including the FBI.

Then, to add to all our misery, we were hit with a lawsuit for $15 million by the deputy sheriff we had charged. The prosecutor was his lawyer, claiming he could represent him because he was not a "full-time prosecutor." It was a direct attempt to get us to back off. It was very intimidating to have such powerful men in the court system coming against us, and now we stood to lose everything we had worked for. This took our focus off the investigation of the prosecutor and deputy prosecutor and intimidated the hell out of us, which was exactly what they were trying to do. We were unable to tell the public the real truth, the truth that this was just another ploy by the officials who were up to their necks in corruption.

We went to court like lambs being led to slaughter. We didn't understand how the prosecutor could represent the very deputy sheriff we were investigating and still be an elected representative who had taken an oath to uphold the law and protect and defend the people. It seemed in Delaware County anything goes if you start rattling the cages of the ones who are raking in the cash illegally. He later got around that with a statement that he was a "part-time prosecutor."

It was an embarrassing time, and, of course, to make it worse, it was front-page news. Seemed as if we were making the front page a lot, but we knew that it was because the corrupt officials had a reporter in their pockets who was always trying to dig up dirt on our department and the administration. We would hide when we saw him coming.

He was a sleazebag with a pen.

One day as I sat in my office, I was approached by a thug who asked me, "How much would it take for you to back off of your investigations?" I was shocked at his temerity and yelled, "There is no amount of money in the world that can buy me. Get the hell out of my office and make sure you tell your friend, the prosecutor, what I said." My little group of men and myself became even more paranoid, watching everything and everyone.

This was not an easy time in my police career. I began longing for the days when I walked the beat or just solved crimes like I did as a detective. But being one of the first women in the state of Indiana to become a police officer and having risen so high in rank, I had to go on as I was afraid I would be letting down the women of the community otherwise. The fact was, some had told me not to resign or back down. *"We need you there,"* they would say. I often wondered where those women were when I needed my house cleaned or my kids taken care of.

CHAPTER SIXTEEN

PERSONAL CHOICES

I began getting a strong following of persons who wanted me to run for sheriff. I thought it over and finally, after a lot of persuasion, I said "yes." During this time, one of my oldest daughters was facing challenges, and I had just taken custody of my baby granddaughter. In less than 24 hours, I had picked her up, baby proofed my house, found a babysitter, and was at work on time.

At our first strategy meeting to send out letters to announce my candidacy, my little granddaughter messed her pants and I went to change her. She was still in diapers and just beginning to babble baby talk. She reached for me and uttered her first recognizable word: "Mimi." That became my name forever after. Even to this day, all her friends and all the grandchildren born after her still call me Mimi.

I realized that I could not go through with running for sheriff. She needed me more than the public needed me to be sheriff. I went back into the room where my friends and volunteers were busy stuffing envelopes and told them my decision. They were all very upset.

"You have to understand that my family comes first. My grand-daughter needs me now, and I have to be there for her," I told them. They all looked sad as they cleaned up the table where they were working, but no one said a word.

Later in the year, I was invited to attend the FBI Academy in Washington, D.C. It would be a six-week stay, but the training and prestige that went along with the school was the most-sought-after in the world. I had to tell them very quickly that I could not take the offer as I had a young baby to take care of. A few years later, she was returned to her mother, but the bond that grew between us was unbreakable. She is the light of my life even to this day. She cares deeply for me and grew into a beautiful young woman with the beauty going clear through to her heart.

My three youngest grandchildren, all girls, are so sweet. They are smart and beautiful, just like my youngest daughter who birthed them. My only grandson makes us all proud. Growing up, for him, was difficult, but he graduated cum laude from college, and he has turned into a wonderful adult who everyone loves. My children and grandchildren are so very precious to me; they mean so much and fill my life with happiness beyond words.

But taking care of my family, combined with the very high stress job on the police department, was really taking its toll. I wanted to rest and could not do so. There were kids to raise, I still had to clock my forty hours a week at the police department, and being on call at night, running an animal shelter, a race track, a farm, plus, I had other responsibilities to members of the community, and keeping our own home in order was overwhelming at times.

My mother was evidently overwhelmed when I was born. There was a lady by the name of Betty who lived across the street from our family who was a nurse and could not have children of her own. My mother would take me over there for her to take care of me. She and her husband became like second parents to me, and I called them Aunt Betty and Uncle Pat. When I was four years old, they adopted a baby through a doctor and named her Susie, but they did not realize until she was three years old that Susie was slightly retarded.

In her later years, Susie became pregnant and had a baby girl she named Lynn. Lynn had something wrong with her and had seizures and could not talk. I stayed close to the family, doing many things for them as they grew older. After Uncle Pat died, Aunt Betty was confined to a wheelchair, and before she died at the age of 92, she had made me guardian over the two women. Aunt Betty left them a three-bedroom house in a nice neighborhood, and they were able to live alone with me overseeing them.

I was responsible for their doctor visits, counseling visits, getting their food, paying their bills, and making sure they kept their house clean. Sometimes the overseeing became a full-time job. It was like having two ten year olds living alone and doing foolish things. Giving them money was not a good thing as they would buy candy, toys, and games, and then call me to say they had nothing to eat. It was frustrating, to say the least. They both became overweight, hated cleaning the house, and did poorly at keeping their hair and body clean. It became a full-time job to keep them going. It only added to my stress level and workload, but they had no one else in the entire world to look after them.

On the farm where we lived I had a small greenhouse where I raised flowers in the spring and summer. That was my only source of relaxation. I loved going over to the greenhouse, and seeing the little seeds spring up and start to blossom brought me much pleasure. Most of my neighbors bought their flowers from me as they were some of the most beautiful flowers in the area. God saw me through all the problems and heavy workload, but my health was beginning to suffer.

CHAPTER SEVENTEEN
FRIENDS LOST

During this time my social life became nil. I didn't seem to have enough time for my friends, something I regret to this day. Most of my friends I have known for over thirty years. Good friends, solid, and there for me whenever I needed them. I always tried to be a good friend to them too, but I did not always succeed.

One of my best friends who worked at the Department of Child Welfare went to the hospital to have a hysterectomy and afterward called me from the hospital to ask me to come visit that evening. We were extremely close and usually talked on the phone every night, telling each other the very latest, bouncing ideas off of each other. I was working my last day before vacation and decided to go home and visit her later in the week. I didn't have the chance. Her sister called me the next day and told me she had thrown a blood clot and had died. I can't even begin to tell how that affected me. Sometimes when your heart is broken, it can never be mended.

I still grieve over her death and perhaps I will never forget the pain as I know her children will forever be affected too. I miss her to this very day, and it has been over twenty years since her death. She left four small children, and later her husband died, leaving the children as orphans. Friends come and go, but the ones that are important in my life will forever play a large part in molding me into the person I am today. God has sent into my life good people, good friends, and given me a passion for people.

I was weary and very discouraged. I had put my life and the lives of my family on the line, kept secrets, made friends for life, and had somehow kept my sanity. But I was tired of watching my back and that of my family. I was paranoid all the time and found myself having too many thoughts of what might have been. *I have worked extra shifts, long hours, been called out in the night for drug cases, and taken terrible risks attempting to curtail the drug traffic in our fair city. What in the crap am I thinking? My priorities should be my two daughters, my home, and my husband, but instead, I am running a fast-pace effort to fight a war on drugs that can never be won.*

After serving twenty-two years in the Muncie, Indiana, Police Department, rising from rookie beat cop chalking tires in the dead of winter, to chief of investigations, I was eligible for retirement, and at forty-five, felt I was still young enough to enjoy a more peaceful life. But the decision to retire from the department was bittersweet. I was leaving behind the only life I had known—the life of a cop. Not just a cop, but an honest one.

PART THREE

CHAPTER ONE

LIFE AFTER RETIREMENT

Back home in Indiana, life resumed at a frantic pace. After our cruise, I had agreed to take on managing the track and animals full time now that I was no longer on the police force. And, as was my style, I was determined to make a success of the track and gave it my all. The race track was run on weekends, and no matter the weather: snow, rain, or sleet, we ran the motocross. I was the ticket seller, standing outside in every kind of weather condition and taking in the fees for the race. The animal shelter was one of the best in the state, adopting out more dogs and cats than the national average.

My husband of forty years and I are farmers, among other things. We cultivate some 500 acres of soy beans and corn and only employ a helper during planting and harvest. When we were raising our two daughters, at times we worked nine full- and part-time jobs between us. My home life during this period was nothing but work and more work. I would come home from working my shift at the police station around four, start dinner, and if it was summertime, go out and mow the four acres around our house. Sometimes night would be descending as I pushed the riding mower faster as I would try to finish the task before it became too dark to see. Living on a farm was wonderful and great for raising our daughters, but the work that went along with it was tremendous.

In time, the track would be profitable for us and fun for Mel, but being in charge of the refreshment stand, tickets, mowing the entire eight acres before each race, making sure all twenty-two employees were there to work, and praying that no one would be hurt as they raced became quite stressful for me.

It was Mel's belief that we should not be in debt to anyone, which meant that we always paid cash for anything we bought, and only bought what we could afford to pay cash for. In theory, it's a great idea, but in reality, it's a killer because of having to work so hard and the toll it takes on your health.

While we were debt free and owned all our possessions outright, my health became an issue with all the stress and work. I told my husband one day … "This ol' mule is tired, and I'm not working as much." This seemed to change his opinion of me as he being an "A" personality could not relate to such a statement. But he didn't object when I told him I wanted to take another trip to Jamaica, by myself.

CHAPTER TWO

RETURN TO JAMAICA

Six months after my first trip to Jamaica, I returned, this time by plane and for four days. As the plane flew over the harbor and made the approach to the Montego Bay Airport runway, the green hills reflecting off the blue sea was as spectacular as I remembered it from my cruise with my family . The familiar scenery brought back the memory of the good time I had in the hills of Jamaica and when the plane touched down at the airport I was eager to get off and start my adventure.

Getting off the plane, the first thing that greets you is the blast of hot air rising from the concrete tarmac. The walk from the plane to the airport terminal, while only a short distance, was an exercise of swimming in moist air and airplane fumes. The terminal was nothing more than an open three-sided metal building with a clock that always said it was 3:00 no matter what day or time you arrived.

The immigration and customs officers moved as if swimming in thick molasses, sweating in the heat that was visibly bouncing off the corrugated steel sheets that made up the immigration and customs hall, the sweat soaking through the thick Oxford cotton shirts and wool trousers and skirts they all wore. As tourists, their examination of our documents and luggage was merely a formality. Only Jamaicans or returning residents were subjected to thorough scrutiny.

After claiming my bags and clearing immigration and customs, I followed the crowd of tourists headed for the outside and stood by the curb, hoping to find a taxi. Unlike my first visit, there was no tour buses lined up, no air-conditioned taxis waiting to transport you wherever you have booked to go. The taxis were Lada station wagons, the sturdy but uncomfortable Russian-made cars that had recently been imported to Jamaica. While they were capable of handling the rough terrain of the Jamaican roads, they were hard on the rear end. But I managed to negotiate a price with a driver and was soon off to the villa where I would be staying for four days.

The villa was a studio apartment in a family-owned development in Montego Bay, and I immediately made friends with a little twelve-year-old girl whose brother worked at the villa as a gardener. He offered to take me with them to visit his family, and I eagerly accepted. The next day, we traveled over an hour straight up a mountain to the little shack they lived in, which was hanging on the side of a mountain, and Karen, the gardener's little sister, was as cute as they come.

The same day I met her I unofficially adopted Karen and would later help to send her to school until she graduated, then on to a college where she boarded and eventually became a teacher. She now teaches in the school she attended, and at age thirty-five is still my "daughter." She has never married because she is waiting for the right Christian man to come along, but her home is so isolated that I have my doubts that she will ever be able to meet a man. But through God and faith, all things are possible.

It was as if God broke my heart for the people during this trip and I spent the four days crying and seeking God, praying as we traveled around the island. I needed to seek God for an answer. And in no time the four days passed, and I returned to Indiana. But months and months after that trip I still could not get the people of Jamaica off my mind. I prayed to God to help me find why I had such a burden for those people. I continued to seek God for answers, and finally I decided to take a walk in faith and return to the island. This time, I packed Bibles, some clothes and shoes to give away, and started my journey in the hills outside of Montego Bay. Now, remember, I really knew nothing about this land, the culture, or the workings of this strange but wonderful place.

It was hard to understand the language as most Jamaicans spoke a patois between themselves, and even those who spoke English really well spoke a kind of broken English. I later developed an ear for the patois, enough so that I can understand what is being said but didn't try to speak it because each time I try, the listeners usually get a good laugh out of it. I had no place to live and no vehicle to get around in but a lot of walking and the help of good friends and a few cabs got me where I needed to go.

I started making more and more frequent trips to Jamaica, and my stays there got longer and longer. I would return to America after being on the island for a few months, but my mind would always return to the poverty that I had seen in the country. It was heartbreaking for me at times, and I know it had to be breaking the heart of God.

After praying about it, I decided to formally establish my ministry in Jamaica and sold my car for $10,000 to get *Jesus for Jamaica* off the ground. God would just have to open the doors that needed to be opened, and that is exactly what He did!

Soon, I began taking friends and family with me on my trips to the island to help provide whatever services we could. Besides, they could help to carry the relief items we brought on our trips. Back then, the planes only flew in once a week, and your return trip had to be scheduled weeks ahead of time.

I so wanted to be used by God to help these people, and at times it was so overwhelming that I could hardly function. I would crash when I went back home to the States, sometimes not leaving the sofa for days. I kept asking why I deserved to live in a country of wealth and prosperity where there is so much waste of everything and other people were born to a condition of complete despair. Being home always highlighted for me that our country is the most wasteful place in the world.

Drugstores are the worse, throwing away the "old" and bringing in new for the shelves. I was able to fill two vans at one such drugstore, personally taking perfectly NEW, still sealed and packaged shampoos, soaps, toothbrushes, deodorant, and household items from Dumpsters that were filled with these items. My team and I would drive the van to the drugstore's parking lot, pull up to the Dumpster, and load the goods into boxes in the back of the vans. We managed to do this a few times until the company caught on to me and started pouring bleach on the items to ruin them. The items I did manage to recover were still good and are a godsend for the poor of Jamaica. I knew there was so much work to be done and very few avenues to receive help. Churches seemed to sit on their pocketbooks in the United States, and money was very hard to raise from donors.

CHAPTER THREE
BEGGAR FOR THE POOR

I became a beggar for the poor. It was an uphill battle everywhere I gave talks. There was always the pat answer for the churches: "We already support outreaches or missionaries," but I was always able to beg enough money to build little houses for the people, run the soup kitchen, and give out clothing to the needy. I believe after God's call, had I not responded, I would be a miserable old lady by now, drying up in the pews of my church which I had attended for twenty-three years, and which I eventually left.

Gee, what can I say about my church in Indiana? I was fed the Word by the church elders and pastor, but my ministry was barely support-ed. It was loved by some of the 400 congregation members, but when our original pastor, teacher, and avid supporter retired, a new admin-istration came into play, and a new game plan was instrumented. Jesus for Jamaica ministry was becoming more and more like a stepchild. It hurt me because the pain and hunger I witnessed every day in Jamaica was part of me and my life as I shared their dilemma. I would pray that the church would catch the vision and stood on Habakkuk 2:2 in the Bible: "Write your vision and make it plain upon tablets that he may run that readeth it."

Things got worse when the last "pastor" took over. Not only were we not being fed the Word of God, but he completely ignored the e-mails and phone calls to get help for our new soup kitchen in Jamaica.

After returning from a long haul in Jamaica where I was seeing such needs, I attended my church on Sunday. The pastor, his already bulky body straining his designer suit even more than usual, looked as if he had gained twenty or thirty pounds since the last time I had seen him when he had refused to give our mission a donation. We had needed to build a house for a family of ten and help put food on their table, plus our food at the soup kitchen was running low.

Looking at his fat, chipmunk cheeks and red, greasy complexion, I could not hold back the anger as I walked up to where he was greeting people. His false, pasted-on smile disappeared as he saw me approaching. I angrily confronted him. "You don't look like you have missed any meals. Why did you not answer my calls about the people in Jamaica going hungry?" I demanded.

When he gave me his standard answer about already supporting other missions, a claim I knew to be a lie, it took all my self-control to not slap his lying mouth. After attending my home church for twenty-three years, that was the last day I went there. I immediately started looking for a new church.

CHAPTER FOUR

THE START OF THE MINISTRY

We originally started the ministry by living in little shacks with outside showers and toilets on a stretch of the beach in Negril. When I first saw the beach, it was candy to the eyes. Majestic palm trees swayed to the trade winds, and the most beautiful sugar-white sandy beaches stretched for miles. The blue water, calm and clear for as far as the eyes could see greeted your eyes.

But, as you know, all that glitters is not gold. While the surroundings are breathtaking, I found it to be a place of utter despair and heartbreak. The beach was full of drug dealers, prostitutes, and nudity was the norm rather than the exception. But it was also a place of hope, joy, and generosity. Some of the most poverty-stricken persons were the most loving and kind to us.

While we had great success with getting people saved and baptized in the Caribbean Sea, things were difficult for our teams. We really never had a place to hang our hats, so to speak. Our accommodations were usually in whatever guesthouse on the beach that I could beg for discounts, and even then it was expensive. That worked for a while, but for some members of the teams that started coming to minister and do outreach, the nudity and sin on the beach was too much to live with day to day. As the teams I began bringing with me to help with the outreach grew in numbers, the issue of housing became critical.

A time came when I was expecting a team and did not have a place to house the groups a few weeks before their arrival. My treks from guesthouses to hotels asking for discounts did not bear much fruit. I was a study in despair, but was determined to find a solution before the full team arrived.

In church back in Indiana where I am from, just as our advance team was getting ready to return to Jamaica—two others would travel with me to plan for the full team—a woman approached me with an envelope of money. She said she had a dream she felt was from God. God told her to give the three of us who would soon journey to Jamaica some money for goats. She said that in the vision she was instructed that the goats would be for a family in a village, and then the newborns were to be given to poor families in a village. She put the envelope with the money in my hands, looked in my eyes, and made me promise that I would ensure things were done exactly as she asked.

When we got on the plane to Jamaica, the only thing we knew was the fact that we were to buy goats and give the offspring to the poor in some unknown village. At that time, I was not familiar with many villages. Vicky and Gene, the couple that were with me, knew nothing about anything, this being their first trip to Jamaica. We were all babes in the woods.

On one of my first mission visits to Negril, I had made friends with Sammy, a gardener at a local guesthouse. He had pledged to me and my friends that he would sit by our side as a friend, as a brother, and that no harm would come to us as long as he was around. Sammy's front teeth were missing, but he had a smile that was contagious. He always came around the beach when we had outreaches.

Soon after arriving at the little place on the beach where we were staying, still without much success in locating housing, the three of us were sitting around talking. Sammy came walking over and greeted us in his normal way. "What you come here to do this time?" he asked, flashing his no-teeth grin.

The last time our outreach team was a group of doctors and dentists. We laughed and told him we were not sure. His response was startling. "I know what you must do. You need to buy some goats so that you can feed the poor. After the newborns are here, you could give them to families in a village."

We all began to weep. Sammy was puzzled at what he might have said to upset us and make us cry. It took some time, but we finally convinced him that our tears were tears of joy. After he calmed down, we told him that he had just repeated the dream that our church sister had back at our church. He fell back in a chair, crying and shaking his head. "Do you mean God is using me?" he said in disbelief. Then by the emphatic shake of his head, he seemed to come to a decision.

"Miss Kit, this is God's will. How could your friend in farin know what I was thinking? You don't see. It is a miracle. So I have decided I going help you. I am going to help you to build a church so that you don't have to continue to preach in Sodom & Gomorrah. I will collect you on Saturday, and we will journey to my village in Hanover where I will give you some family land to build a church and raise goats." Sammy hired a driver and took us to the family land, and there, on the side of a beautiful mountain, he presented us with land.

We were floating on air. We could not believe our ears and burst out crying again and thanking God for the miracle we had just witnessed. God was showing us the way to do exactly what He wanted us to do.

CHAPTER FIVE

BASE CAMP

During the time we ministered without a home, sometimes we would sleep on school floors or in the already crowded small shanty homes of the Jamaicans. We couldn't all sit together for a meal. In my quiet moments, I would visualize a place where the entire group could all sit around a big table, fellowshipping and eating our meals together instead of being scattered, always scrambling to find a suitable place on the beach to eat.

A "base camp" would be so nice I told myself and God. We had paid our dues, and I know that God could see that and would bless us for all the sacrifices we had made in order to serve Him. We had learned so much along the way about the culture, the people, and the hardships here in Jamaica, and had we not walked in their footsteps, I don't believe we could have learned it so easily.

Come Saturday morning, we set out traveling around to the South Coast of Jamaica. We had no car, so we traveled by minibus and taxi. I'm sure you can imagine that we were quite a sight. It was an all-day proposition, and our destination could not be reached before nightfall. Therefore, we needed to find a place to stay for the night. As night began to fall, I became anxious. I did not know exactly where we were or where we were headed. Mel had traveled with me to Jamaica and this was the first time we had ventured out from Negril. We had planned a trip across the mountains to an orphanage to help some of the children. We realized that we could not make it to Brownstown before nightfall and decided to stop where we could find a room for the night.

We found a guesthouse on the beach and decided we would rest there overnight and continue our journey the next day. As we sat on the guesthouse porch in the evening, admiring the views that were unbelievable, the untouched beauty of the south coast was awesome. The area was clearly untouched by tourists and the usual tourist traps and still maintained its spectacular, natural beauty.

The following day after a night sleeping to the sounds of the waves crashing on the rocks, I asked the owner where we were. I was pleasantly surprised when he said we were just outside of Whitehouse. "Oh, I know that village," I said, much to his surprise.

"You really know Whitehouse, Miss Kit? How come?" he asked, clearly skeptical.

"Yes. I came here on a tour the very first time I visited Jamaica."

Later as we were enjoying coffee on the veranda, I overheard the waitress talking to the cook about a house that was for rent next door. I quickly asked about it and prayed as I walked next door to inquire about the rental. The lady, known as Sister, was happy to show me the house. It had been in her family for years, and she was anxious to rent it out. I walked into the first room and saw windows clear across the front facing the Caribbean Sea. What a beautiful sight, then lo and behold … there in the middle of the room was the table and chairs that I had envisioned for our teams. I knew immediately that it was to be our "base camp."

We used this house for three years as a place to bring teams but soon were outgrowing it. It had three bedrooms, but could only sleep seven people. Our teams were now beginning to number eighteen to thirty people. We started looking for another facility that could house more people.

CHAPTER SIX

FINDING A NEW BASE CAMP

Housing in Jamaica is difficult and on the south coast nearly impossible. I knew if we were to continue with the outreach we had to find something decent to live in. I had made contact with a person who told me about a woman that could help us with a rental.

When the villa manager arrived, I immediately recognized Marge Ball, our lunch hostess from my first visit with Mel. As we both fell into each other's arms, me laughing and crying at the same time, and she a little bewildered but nevertheless warm, I was sure it was ordained by God.

Marge became a close friend, not only with advice for the ministry, but her knowledge of the area. She had built over 600 houses and owned hundreds of acres of land, some on the beach. She was the overseer for a vacant villa, neglected and run-down but sitting on a lovely piece of land facing the sea. When she took me to see it, we had to pull ourselves up the crumbled steps and the house was even a worse mess. Goats and rats had taken over the place. The grass was tall and bushy all around. The only person occupying the premises was an old fisherman who lived in the basement.

When I first saw it all overgrown by high grass I turned to Miss Ball and said, "Get me out of here." She just laughed at me and said that she would get her men to come and do repairs and painting and THEN ... I could look at it again. She always had an answer and with her mild manner, you felt that she could perform magic.

The old fisherman was living in the lower part of the villa. He introduced himself as "Cleophas Sandbrows the caretaker," and he politely informed us that he was not a squatter but had lived there all his life and had been given legal authority by the owners.

I quickly reassured him that we had no intention of asking him to leave and hoped that we would be good friends.

It took a week to do the necessary repairs and paint the walls of the old villa on the Whitehouse coast. Believe me, it took a lot of hard work to get it clean from all the goat smells, but we did and the place sparkled with the blue Caribbean Sea as our backyard.

The first morning after we moved into the villa, I fixed my pot of Blue Mountain coffee and sat on the bright window seat cushion I had sewn for the bedroom seat, savoring the great taste and flavor of what is for sure, the best coffee in the world. I gazed out the window toward the sea. This was about 5:30 in the morning. I am an early riser.

As I looked out the window, I saw Mr. Sandbrows walking with a rusty tin can in his hands. I observed that he would walk to various trees in the yard and empty his rusty can. After a couple of days observing this, I got up the nerve to ask him what he was doing every morning when I saw him in the garden.

That was when I learned that he had no toilet in his downstairs apartment and normally would relieve himself in the bushes during the daytime, but at night he used a small, old, rusty can. Each morning, he was emptying what he had passed during the night. That very day, I called a plumber to put some plumbing in his little room. He was forever grateful and from that day on, we became close friends.

With a lot of work, I was able to bring the villa back to life. Mr. Sandbrows and I would go into the bush to scrounge for plants and flowers. And with the wild orchids and wild flowers that we found and a yard that was finally mowed and groomed, it looked like the tropical paradise it is. It was a place of beauty. The views from the windows were spectacular; a million-dollar view of the bay and the mountains.

When he died some years later in his little apartment, it was very hard for me. Mr. Sandbrows and I had become more than best of friends. He was my Jamaican papa and spiritual counselor. I cried so hard at his funeral and would not go up to the casket to view his thin and old body. I couldn't, and I wanted to remember him as I had grown to know him——sitting under the giant guango tree in the yard, weaving fishnets with the sun filtering through the tree's leaves onto his white dreadlocked hair that looked like the guango's hanging roots. I wanted to remember him coming and going in his little dugout canoe and how happy he was when he caught enough fish to feed himself and sell a few. His life had been hard, and now he was at rest in heaven with all the fish he would ever need.

After he died, his apartment became the start of our outreach to provide a home for some of the street boys. I started with fivethree boys we took in from their life on the street.

Bim Bim was the first of five boys. Bim Bim stole my heart from the beginning.

CHAPTER SEVEN

MAKING NEW FRIENDS

The base camp where I lived for fourteen years when I am in Jamaica and where we brought teams to stay was at the same old villa I had rented. In the bottom of the base camp was where we began our outreach mission with homeless boys by providing a safe place for them to live. This was the apartment where Mr. Sandbrows lived until he died.

It was not a basement but had low ceilings and was a little on the dark side, and it felt like you were in a basement. It had a bathroom and two bedrooms. It was small but for the boys so much better than their conditions at home or living on the street. We put bunk beds and a couple of single beds in the rooms and most times had as many as six young boys living there. All were encouraged to attend church, and it was a proud day when they chose to be baptized.

One of the boys who had been put on the street because his family could not feed him was unable to talk. "Rat," as he was known, just made grunting sounds. We found that he had a grandmother living high in the mountains, so Elaine,my friend since teenage days who was helping with the ministry, and I decided to walk up the mountain and talk to her.

After hours of climbing straight up an incline and hanging onto vines to aid our climb, we came to a shanty on the side of a ravine. That is where we found "Rat's" grandmother. She had her head wrapped in a blue scarf and was missing most of her teeth. The shanty was leaning to the left, and we could see the inside through the boards. She was tending to a fire where it seemed she was cooking something. She was using old paint cans for her cooking pots. The fire was only a few feet from the shanty.

The view from this part of the rugged mountain was stunning. I was amazed that anyone could live this high in the mountains and survive. We asked her a question, and to our amazement, she too grunted her words. Elaine and I looked at each other and wondered if this trip had been in vain. Come to find out that is how they communicated in that family.

While we talked, she responded with what sounded to us like grunted words. We still did not yet have much of an ear for the local patois. But in the end, we managed to make out that she was giving her consent to take Rat off the street. Elaine and I headed back down the mountainside feeling as if we had gone back in time to the age where words had not been formed into a known language, maybe even back to the caveman days!

We took the five boys back to the base camp, including Rat, and fed them until their bellies were full. Sam, who had come down to help with the ministry, cut their hair and we made sure they had a good bath. The next day, we purchased new school uniforms for them and drove them to school to make sure that they arrived there. As we drove through the village of Whitehouse, they hung out the windows yelling at everyone they knew. They were proud to be normal, or at least as normal as they could be for now.

CHAPTER EIGHT
BOYS AT THE BASE CAMP

The boys were thriving, and we all had fallen in love with their antics. They were taught to pray, to respect each other, and to be obedient to their elders. I was due to go home and was worried about who would take care of the boys while I was gone. I also had a kitten we called TT which I had rescued from a dark bar where she was tied with rope. The bartender said that was the only way a cat could be trained. I was so upset and kept asking him for the kitten. Finally, I offered him a shirt as a trade and TT went home with me to the base camp. Now, I was in need of a sitter for the boys and a kitten.

I began walking from house to house, asking if they knew anyone who would help with the boys. It seemed hopeless; I kept praying and telling God … that I can't leave this island until I find someone who is willing to take over my responsibilities here. God knew that the need was urgent, and therefore, answered my cry once again.

Miss Sadie was a helper in the next villa beside the base camp. She could not have children, but had a loving heart. She agreed to oversee the boys while I was in the States, cooking for them, praying with them, and making sure they did the chores. She was a delightful woman. She became my best friend, sister, prayer partner, and confidante, and many a time an encourager when things got tough in the ministry.

It was hard at times trying to take care of so many needs and problems. When I would be overwhelmed with things, I would tell myself, it's not about me; these are God's people. I'm just here to help. I would give it to God and wait for a while. It seemed to work, sometimes not as quickly as I would think it should, though. That's when I would find Miss Sadie and we would pray, usually under the big guango tree, and the problem seemed to be resolved. It was evident that God was in control of all the good that was manifesting. I realized that God would take care of things if I trusted Him.

Ninja was a difficult young man to understand. His temper got the best of him at times. He followed me around like a puppy and waited on me hand and foot, telling me that he would die for me. I was thirty years his senior, but his love for me was unshakable and unbelievable. I believed he saw in me a mother, a friend, and a sister. I tried to help him to learn how to get along in life and always provided him with jobs that came along.

We trained Ninja to drive and coached him so that he could apply for a driver's license. He was able to pass the test and began driving for our teams, picking them up at the airport, driving them to the worksites and for their day of play at the beach. It took a large load off of me, and things seemed to be going well. The ministry had taken off to the point that we were building two or three houses a year, digging pits for bathrooms, constructing a school, and then a large clinic. We needed a project manager, someone who knew the building codes, how to string electrical wires, plumb buildings, and do cement work. The ministry ended up building quite a few houses for people on the mountain, and Ninja became our construction foreman as his knowledge became apparent with each building project.

At one point when his temper got the better of him and he ended up in jail for stabbing another man in a fight, I made him stay away from the mission and the base camp for over a year, and that seemed to be a wake-up call for him to change. When he came back, everyone told me not to give him another chance, but not only do I believe in second chances, I don't believe in throwing the baby out with the bathwater. He seems changed now and has become very productive.

CHAPTER NINE
BUNNIE & BIM BIM

Bunnie was fifteen years old and so skinny and hungry, it took weeks to get him filled with food. He had been living on the street, and we had met at a little church in the mountains. He had gone to the front of the church and prayed out loud for God to find him a place to lay his head and put food on his plate. I was so touched by his prayer that I ask the pastor if I could take him to the base camp. Bunnie was ever so thankful for a roof over his head and food. He began getting taller and stronger. He helped to take care of the base camp when I was in the States, mowing and raking the three acres surrounding the camp. He loved being a part of the ministry. He taught himself to play the guitar and would keep us all uplifted in prayer and song.

He was a good student, and when he finished at the All-Age School all the boys attended, we got the chance to send him to a boarding school on the North Coast, where he would finish his schooling and be taught a trade. We put him on a truck that was headed that way, along with his meager belongings, and except for school vacations, Bunnie did not return to the base camp. He attended school for three years. He was taught cabinet making during his time at the school and eventually graduated from there.

The boys stayed close to me when I returned, but Bim Bim stayed the closest. Bim was my kid, and he stayed by my side as he grew. He was always small for his age but eager to please everyone. Although he was not my birth child, I felt as close to him as I did my own two daughters.

The mission had started to build houses for the people in the village, and I was able to help his mother and sister obtain a little house.

Bim was very ambitious and tried everything he could do to help the family. He seemed to think even as a young boy that his responsibility was to earn a living for his family. We were able to help his mother, brother, and two sisters with a small house.

He began spearing fish, diving down to find the best fish he could spear. He would then sell the fish and have some extra money for the family. Seeing him work so hard for little money, I decided to support the family. I was able to do that until I found out a year later that Bim Bim's mother had been offered two jobs but turned them down, one a job hand washing clothes and the other to take care of a young baby. I was supporting the family, but I realized that I was not "helping" by making her lazy.

Bim stayed at the base camp on and off. Early one morning he came to the base camp and asked to have a talk with me. He was all of eighteen years old and still the size of a twelve year old. He was there to tell me that he was going to be a father. I was so disappointed in him; I immediately started lecturing him about the sad state he would be in as a young father. He hung his head in shame, not looking at me or saying a word as I spoke. And after I was finished, his only answer to me was "Everyone makes mistakes."

I did not see him again until after the baby boy was born, and he again visited me early one morning. He showed me a small bottle that was empty. He asked me if I would buy some medicine for the baby as he was running a fever. I was still upset at him and refused to help.

"Bim, I have supported your family for nine years. You are a man now, and I won't start again with your family. You have to be responsible for this child, not me." He turned around and left the base camp. That would be the last time I would see him alive.

While he lived with me, I had always forbidden Bim to go to the outer banks to fish on the large boats. The journey was 100 miles out, and the men on the keys were like pirates. The talk was that they were thieves. People said that they had run away from the law and were living in little shacks on the keys. I found out that Bim had left for a five-day trip on a large boat. I lay awake most of the night as the seas were rough and I could hear a storm approaching. I prayed and prayed for his safety and when he returned, I gave him a stern warning. He was only fourteen-years-old at that time and had no business going with the older fishermen to the outer banks.

On a beautiful May day while I was home in Indiana, I received a phone call. Bim had been murdered. I fell to the floor, sobbing after I heard the details. A few weeks after I left for the States, he had gone back out to sea to fish, and he did the one thing I had forbidden him to do. He went to the keys to fish, and it was there that he was murdered. He had been diving with an air hose, and a fisherman who was angry with him had cut the air hose. There were five witnesses, but none would come forward with the truth when the police took over the case. In Jamaica, you see nothing and you hear nothing or you would end up the same as the deceased.

I left the States immediately for Jamaica, but by the time I got here, his funeral was over. Some 1,000 people had attended his funeral. That speaks volumes about his popularity in the community. I miss Bim Bim, and even to this day I wonder what he would be like as an adult. Sometimes the things we do or don't do come back to haunt us. Bim's death threw me into a deep depression. He was a fine young man, and I felt that if I had only given him the money he needed, he would still be alive.

CHAPTER TEN

THE FRUITS OF OUR MINISTRY

There were other boys who came occasionally to the base camp, and sometimes it could get crowded. Of course, sometimes this presented problems. Some of them came to us with illnesses. One such case was Mark. Mark was ten years old and had been left on the street by his father, who told him he would be back at Christmas to get him. Well, Christmas came and went, and a year later, still no signs of his father. When I heard about Mark, I invited him to stay at the base camp.

A couple of days after he arrived, while I was preparing for a team that was arriving the following week to help with outreach, I noticed that Mark was looking a little peaked.

When I looked closer at the ten year old, I realized that his eyes were yellow. I knew right away that he had hepatitis. I made a frantic call to the team leader, and the team trip was cancelled. Keeping Mark away from the others was almost impossible, but God worked it out that no one else came down with the dreaded disease.

We, as humans, should realize that everything is in God's timing, but being a woman, I get very anxious and want to see manifestations of His work immediately, which I have over and over. Maybe I'm spoiled now, seeing God work so many times and thinking each prayer must be answered in "MY" time. That is just not the way He works. I realize that His thoughts are not like our thoughts; that it is only by His grace and mercy that we *can* choose to be with Him in heaven. I know that I am no more than a dirty rag, and that His favors and miracles are not because I do what I do, but because of His dying on the cross for us, and because He loves us; a very simple lesson, and we should keep that in our being and spirit all the time, but we fall short of His glory continually.

There were other street boys that we "adopted," and most are now doing okay. One, Damion, who I thought would never have a future, is the most successful, working as a lifeguard at a large hotel. He seems as happy as a young man could be in Jamaica.

I met Damion the same day with his friends and brother Bim Bim. I was walking on a deserted beach that was near our new base camp. I saw three little boys swimming, holding on to a piece of floating board. I called to them and began a conversation. When they came out of the water, they were as naked as the day they were born. They looked to be no older than seven or eight years.

After they had put on their clothes, if you could call them clothes since they consisted of a waistband with some rags hanging from the band and tattered T-shirts that had long since lost any distinctive color, I started engaging in conversation with them. I learned that they were living on the street, stealing food and fruit off the trees wherever they could find it. They were using rocks as toilet paper and sleeping wherever they could find shelter. I told them they could come to our base camp, and we would give them food and shelter.

Paulas and Aston learned block laying and cement work. Adian and Adrean learned building tactics, and Chang, our baby, just loved to sing and show off. He was fifteen, but the size of a nine-year-old. We babied him too much, but isn't that what you do to the youngest of the family? Yes, we were, and continue to be, a family, and although some are grown up with families of their own and have left the camp, they still keep in touch with me and each other.

CHAPTER ELEVEN

SOME DISAPPOINTMENTS

I soon began inviting groups of people, including from universities, to join the cause which I had named *Jesus for Jamaica*. Before long and over the years, some 700 persons had heard the call and joined me on the mission field. Some came to stay, and some came for a week or two, but much was accomplished and people's lives were changed, both by the ones who came and the Jamaicans who we were ministering to. People from all walks of life heard the call and responded; this included pastors, dentists, doctors, university professors, as well as ordinary citizens and teens.

Not everybody that came had charity and altruism in their hearts. Most were here to serve and help, but there were some that looked at it as a tropical vacation. Some of the so-called "pastors" came with their own agenda, criticizing the way the local churches were operating in Jamaica. They did not understand the local native religious practices like Pocomania, and some of the more, shall we say, "vigorous" styles of worship, and felt that the African influences in some churches were pure witchcraft. But I for one felt we were here to teach, set examples, and uplift. Many times I was disappointed in the things I observed in people.

Sometimes people can be so cruel and maybe not even realize how they are hurting others. The people I have as helpers are my closest friends. They are ones who have served by my side for many years, some as long as I have been on the south coast of Jamaica. They are loyal and true, and I was very surprised at the attitudes of some of the people that came.

One of the team leaders brought many teams throughout the

years; he was always given free housing and food as an honorarium for his help. He became a good one to bounce ideas off about the ministry and was at one time the president of our board of directors. But as time went by, he became selfish, seemingly ignoring our ministry but still coming for the freebies from us. On his visits he never brought gifts for me and other members of the mission, but he had favorite people he would bring gifts for. Basically, he treated our helpers with little regard.

The tipping point came one day when he went out with a team. They had traveled all day, stopping in places to offer medical assistance in small villages. When they stopped to get refreshments, he bought sodas for everyone who was riding in the van, but our Jamaican driver was never offered any. This made me lose my respect for him, and that was sad as I had believed he loved the Jamaican people and was a servant of God. He had insulted my helpers, and now he was hurting me. When one of them is hurt, I feel it deeply, sort of like when one of your kids gets kicked in the face.

CHAPTER TWELVE
EXPANDING THE MISSION

One evening I had driven to the local bakery with a friend to have some ice cream. As I parked the car, I was surrounded by twelve men, some young, others older. I rolled up the windows as I felt afraid of them, but immediately I felt bad. I rolled down the window a little to hear what they were saying to me.

"Miss, Miss, we are very hungry," they all said in unison. When I asked how come they were all there at the same time and hungry, the reply was that Mr. Babe was out of town, and they could not get any bread to eat, and therefore, all were hungry. Mr. Babe is the owner of the local wholesale bakery. He would give leftover bread to them.

I went home that evening, praying to God and telling Him that no one should be hungry and pleaded for Him to give me an answer. The answer came a few days later when the thought from God was that I should start a soup kitchen. We had been leasing a 100-year-old house on the main street of the village. We had started a computer school which was doing well. Computers were new to the island, and young people were eager to learn the workings of computers.

We converted one side of the house into a soup kitchen, and it took off like lightning. People from the street and nearby villages came by the dozens. A lot of the people were elderly. People were hungry, but they were also hungry for the Word of God. We began with singing and praising God, then someone, possibly a pastor, would bring forth the Word. If we had relief items to give out, we would then give toothpaste, soap, food, and if we had extra rice or flour we gave that too. I can't begin to tell you how the mother in me was satisfied, seeing the poor being cared for and fed a hot meal. Many of the street people became my friends; they were all living and sleeping wherever they could find something to shield them from the night dew.

Joy, a lady who had been on the street for years and who sometimes wore underpants on her head, brought laughter to me each time we talked. She was very intelligent and gave somewhat good advice to all who would stop and get to know her.

Reggie had been sleeping on the street when someone poured gasoline on him and set him on fire. He lived but was a cripple since that day. We were able, with the help of others, to build him a small house on his sister's land. Each day, Reggie walks miles from his home back down to the village to beg for money.

Ricky had so much talent and could sing and outpray most pastors but had wasted his life living on the street. Cocaine is so easy to get and cheap to buy. Ricky had used it for years and looked much older than he was. I worried that we would find him dead sometime as we had others who lived and died on the street. I loved them all. I worried about their health and their well-being just as if they were my own kids. Sometimes I wondered if I was the only one that did care for them.

CHAPTER THIRTEEN

NEW CHALLENGES

I had always stayed in the base camp with teams or alone when the teams left. But it was really starting to get to me, "burned-out" some call it or something to that affect. My day at the base camp would usually start before I could have my first cup of coffee or finish my morning prayers. People came needing food, clothes, prayer, medicine, help for toothaches, boils, cuts, infections, you name it. Because they could not afford a doctor, they would run to me, and God gave me the ability to use my hands for their healing, whether by prayer or by the supplies I had on hand.

I remember early one morning, Mr. Kelly was sitting under a tree in the front yard of the base camp when I woke. Mr. Kelly was 68 years old, or so he thought, and had been hit by a car, breaking his leg. When the doctor put the pieces back in place, his leg was set crooked and healed that way. He slept in the bush on the mountain, which was very hard on a man his age, but Mr. Kelly loved the rum and whenever he could, he partook of a swig to "ease di pain."

"Good mawnin', Miss Kit," he greeted me, the white rum fumes coming off him, almost overwhelming me as I went up to him. "I been going to di crusade over in di other village, Miss Kit, and I had attended faithfully for three weeks straight," he said. "Miss Kit, I need a suit and dress shirt for the last night of the crusade," he declared. *I wanna get saved and give up drinking and living the life I'm liven.*

As part of the mission, I would collect donations of new and used clothing from stores, church members, and other donors in America, and would have my friends and family bring them in whenever they came. We stored them in our base camp to give out when necessary.

I knew I had nothing in the storage room of donated clothing that would be appropriate for him. But I checked the clothes anyway and could not even find a dress shirt. He was very disappointed, and so was I when I told him, "Mr. Kelly, I can't find anything for you." He left, but that was not the end of it for him.

The next day when I came out early in the morning, Mr. Kelly was there under the mango tree again, asking me once more for a suit. I tried not to show my annoyance as I told him emphatically, "Mr. Kelly, I don't have a suit for you!" But he would not be swayed.

"Please, Miss Kit, find a suit of clothes for me. I know you can do it. Check again, Miss Kit," he pleaded.

I figured the only way to get him to leave was to look again and prove to him that I did not have a suit, so I went back into the storeroom and there, hanging in the corner, was a suit, white dress shirt, vest, and pants. I was overjoyed and went running to where Mr. Kelly was sitting, yelling, "Praise God, Mr. Kelly. Here is a suit. I didn't see it before!"

Mr. Kelly smiled as he tried on the suit in the yard. It fit him as if it had been tailor-made for him. His face was creased in a smile of wonder as he said, "Our God gives us the desires of our hearts, Miss Kit, and He knew Mr. Kelly was indeed in need of a fine suit of clothes. What a mighty God we serve!" Mr. Kelly went to the last night of the crusade and proudly gave his life to the Lord.

As the years passed, I found myself being doctor, nurse, counselor, friend, mother, and surgeon. It became a full-time job, even though sometimes only the simplest of things could be done; yet, it made a tremendous difference in someone's life.

One Sunday evening, a young lady came to my gate asking for help; her face on the left side was swollen, and she had a terrible toothache from an infected tooth.

Knowing we could not find a doctor or dentist for days, I took a look in her mouth. Her gums were swollen to the point of bursting,

and surrounding the infected tooth was a pus-filled boil. I told my
helper to find a needle, cotton balls, peroxide, and flashlight. I prayed
that God would help me with this, and had the helper hold the flashlight to give me a better view as I looked in her mouth.

I put a match to the needle and lanced the gum, releasing the pus
and draining the infection, and gave her four ibuprofen tablets, then
sent her home. Three days later when she came back to the base camp,
the swelling was gone and her face was normal. She greeted me with
a big smile. "Thanks, Miss Kit. Mon, that wonder drug you give me
took all di pain away."

I laughed to myself as I told her, "God had just performed another
one of His miracles."

CHAPTER FOURTEEN

REALITY BITES

I soon realized that when you are living or staying in a third world country, you rely on God a lot more. In the United States, most people don't realize it, but we really don't need anything. Everything is available at our fingertips, and most people think they don't need God much. They only call on Him when they are in a pickle or sick or someone they love is sick.

In Jamaica, I needed Him every hour as sometimes we would find ourselves in situations that were so intense, so dangerous. Often, I couldn't understand why people did certain things, so I would call out in prayer for protection. It was different from my years on the force. Then, all I had to do was pick up the radio mike and call for help.

One couple, Polly and Jon, along with their three children, came to Jamaica on a team. They stayed at our base camp for a week and ministered with us on McAlpine Mountain. At the end of their week in Jamaica, they told me that they felt God was calling them to come full time to Jamaica and had decided to answer the call. They went home and sold all their worldly possessions, used the money to buy basic necessities for themselves and their children, packed a container, and six months later, returned to the island.

They found a small house to rent a few blocks from our base camp and began taking in children from the street. This served to ease some of the pressure on the base camp, since we now had another place for street children. Soon, word got around and more and more mothers and grandmothers began to send their children to the orphanage. It was not unusual for a mother to offer her child to an American, believing that the child would have a better life. Many mothers can't feed

LINDA BOTKIN

their children and feel that it was better to give them to a white person who they feel can raise them and give them everything she can't.

Polly and Jon began with ten to fifteen children, with the number rising to twenty-four at one time. The house they had rented was small and not equipped for raising so many children, but they put bunk beds in all the rooms and took in as many children as showed up on their doorstep.

There was a very large mansion on the seaside, across the street from their cottage, and word was that it was for sale for $800 thousand million. It was owned by a mysterious Russian man who came to the house for only a couple a weeks each year; the other fifty weeks it stood unoccupied. The house had nine bedrooms, ten bathrooms, several living rooms and dining rooms, a playroom, an Olympic-size swimming pool,. Polly felt it was just what they needed for all the children, and when they saw the Russian gentleman who owned the house arrive for his annual visit, they walked over and introduced themselves.

After telling him about the work they were doing with the children in the village and surrounding communities, Jon asked him if the house was still for sale. The Russian confirmed that he still had it on the market but had not been able to close any sale. He told them that he had, in fact, received two offers, but when the time came to conclude the deal, each of the buyers had mysteriously backed out. Polly and Jon offered him 2 hundred thousand dollars for the house. They didn't have a dime to their names but had faith that he would see the worthiness of the cause and take less, and maybe they could raise the money. The Russian laughed at their offer and said he would think about it.

A year later, they were contacted by a lawyer who told them that the Russian had decided to donate the house to them. When Polly asked what had accounted for his generosity, the lawyer told her that it was more profitable to the Russian to donate the house to them rather than take $money for it.2 . If he donated the house, he would get a sizable tax write-off, while selling the house to them would mean additional tax liability. Never ones to look a gift horse in the mouth, Polly and Jon were overjoyed and moved full throttle to relocate their orphanage into the mansion. They always wondered why the other two potential buyers, who were never identified, couldn't complete the sales.

They operated the orphanage for eleven years with many children taken in who had been living in terrible circumstances. And then the strangest things started to happen. A whispering campaign started in the village against the ministry and Jon and Polly. Jamaicans we would meet in the village, who were usually friendly and helpful, began to avoid them or look away when they met them. When I sent Ninja to find out what the problem was, I was shocked and disappointed. A wealthy Jamaican lady who I had considered to be my friend and who lived not far from the orphanage and helped us at our soup kitchen had begun a campaign to slander the ministry that Jon and Polly had worked so hard to establish.

It soon became apparent that she was a racist and wanted to run all the whites out of the area. She began attacks against our ministry and went so far as to verbally attack a white doctor that lived near me. She took her campaign further by having meetings with the other affluent neighbors in the village to help her cause.

It was a shock for me when I realized that it was racial discrimination that was at play. It was a new thing for me, and I was angry until I thought about it and realized that black people had been subjected to racism by whites for centuries, and it made me able to sympathize with how blacks must have felt in the years they were so wrongly treated and abused. God says to love our enemies and not just our friends, but sometimes it is hard to love one another as He desires. The greatest thing about God is how He can turn evil into something good. With a lot of prayer and nonjudgment toward this woman, she mellowed out and started good works in the community. We became friends again, and we help each other when needed. A lovely ending to a volatile situation.

CHAPTER FIFTEEN
TRAGEDY STRIKES

I began making Jamaican friends that watched my back. In fact, sometimes, they watched too closely. The ones that I began to trust were people I knew would lay down their lives for me, and most times, they were able to keep those with evil intent away from our groups, and so everywhere we went, they tagged along. In the first years of ministry, we walked everywhere, and I know we looked strange to most of the villagers we met, this ragtag group of Jamaicans and the "whities." It seemed we had a large entourage of Jamaicans, both male and female, that walked everywhere we went.

One of the devoted friends was Marge, my very first friend in Jamaica, who was moving full speed ahead with her land development that she had told me about on my very first visit to Jamaica. She encouraged me to buy a piece of land on the beach side in her development telling me, "The land is going to increase in value more than threefold, and prime beach land is getting scarce worldwide." I am glad I listened to her. I had done well with my investments in the United States and was able, years later when living at the base camp became too much for me, to build and pay for my little dream cottage in Jamaica. The cottage was on the beach with a view to die for. I designed it, supervised the building of it, and furnished it with native bamboo furniture. Ninja planted the garden.

One Christmas night, Marge's daughter Daynee-Anne was in a terrible car wreck on the road and was taken to the hospital in Savannah La Mar which was the nearest one to our village of Whitehouse. The hospital in Savannah La Mar had an "open door" policy. There were no doors and anyone or anything can walk in. I have seen chickens and goats walking up and down the wards. Families were expected to bring their own sheets, towels, and pillows for patients in the hospital, and the only way to guarantee that your loved one will eat is to bring food for the patient three times a day. When the hospital gets crowded, it was not unusual for two patients to be in one bed.

The last time I had visited the hospital, the nurses told me they were so short of supplies, they were washing their rubber gloves and hanging them on the line to dry. The nurses in Jamaica's health system are very dedicated, working long hours for very little pay. At the time, they were making less than $100 U.S. per month.

The hospital, which was woefully understaffed and ill-equipped, could not help Daynee-Anne, and she was airlifted by the Jamaica Defense Force helicopter to the Kingston Public Hospital, the Caribbean's largest trauma and critical care hospital. This hospital was even more pathetic.

Daynee-Anne's kidneys had failed, and the only dialysis machine on the island was not working. Even the x-ray machine was broken down. But thankfully, they had one respirator, and it was available. She was placed on the respirator.

A couple days later there was a knock at my door one night at 10:30. Daynee-Anne's cousin was standing at my door crying so hard I could hardly understand her. "Kit, you have to stop them. I know you can do it. You have to help her. You must!"

I handed her a glass of water and managed to calm her down some.

"They are going to take Daynee off the respirator. They say that someone else has been admitted that needs the respirator more than she does. But I know, Kit, that she will die if she is off the respirator. Kit, please call the United States and have a respirator delivered quickly in order to save Daynee-Anne."

I felt completely helpless knowing that there was no way I could have a respirator delivered overnight. It also made me angry to know that had she been in our country, none of this would have happened.

Our country is so blessed with modern medical know-how, and our hospitals have the equipment they need.

Daynee-Anne, the only child of my friend, Marge, and her doctor husband, died later that week, too young and beautiful to leave this world but nonetheless, she had made a lasting impression on all who knew her. Even though it was impossible to airlift a respirator to Kingston to help Daynee-Anne, a year later, our ministry raised enough funds that I was able to have three respirators donated to hospitals in Jamaica and relief items delivered to the hospital along with other medical supplies. The nurses cried when they saw the items we donated. They were all given basic medical supplies like disposable gloves, cotton pads, gauze, bandages, and syringes that they so desperately needed.

CHAPTER SIXTEEN

NEW VISION

Daynee-Anne's death determined the next outreach the ministry would pursue. I decided that our ministry would build a medical clinic and equip it with the best and most up-to-date equipment and technology we could find.

The village where we had built our school was very isolated from the real world. There were only a few houses that were wired for electricity, and the residents had to walk two miles down the mountain for water. They bathed in a river and washed their clothes on rocks in the river, hanging them on branches to dry.

Early in our ministry, there was war on the mountain between two factions fighting for control over the church that practiced Pocomania, the traditional African religious practice that had been brought to Jamaica by the slaves.

Things had gotten so bad that the police came and locked the church with padlocks. I took it on myself to try to mediate by having a meeting with the community. Most of the people turned out because they wanted things settled. The problem is that they had no idea how to hold a proper meeting. They hung in the windows when the building filled up, and everyone was talking at once. At one point, a scuffle broke out in the middle of the room, and an old lady began hitting everyone over the head with her cane.

I almost fled out the back door, but I yelled above the crowd and told them to sit down and shut up. I also told them they had to learn how to settle things without all the confusion and fighting or I would not be back. They finally settled down and the next meeting a couple of weeks later was much calmer. A few more meetings under their belts and they learned to raise their hands to speak, and a year later, had elected officers and formed a community club. Their differences had been settled, and peace came to the mountain village. These people lacked understanding of how civilization works, but their yearning to learn was prevalent, and they were good students. Eighteen years later, I somehow wished they had stayed as innocent and childlike as the day we first came to the village.

One day when we had a team visiting from the United States, I walked to a section of land that lay behind the school we had built for the village. It was a beautiful spot, 2,000 feet above sea level, overlooking the Caribbean Sea. It was like looking down from an airplane. I thought that it would be a wonderful spot to build a clinic in honor of Daynee-Anne, and I called the team together and some of the villagers and together, we joined hands and prayed over the land. We prayed that we would be able to obtain the land for a clinic to be built.

Later that week, I thought to myself, well, we prayed, now it is time to believe. I ordered 600 cement blocks to be delivered to the middle of the land we had prayed over. It is very difficult to deliver anything up the mountain because it is steep and has lots of curves. I have seen many a truck attempting to carry building materials up the mountain and have to dump their load before arriving at the intended site. But our blocks were delivered safe and sound.

CHAPTER SEVENTEEN

CONFRONTATION

A few days later, I saw a small red car in the village. The man at the wheel was calling all the men in the village over to his car. When they went over, he got out of the car and began waving his hands, cursing and yelling. He then jumped into his car and drove off in a squeal of tires and flying dust and pebbles. After he left, the men came running to me.

"Miss Kit, that was a man from UDC," they explained. The Urban Development Commission, or UDC, was the arm of the government responsible for the use and development of government lands and property. Their reputation in Jamaica was usually tied to scandal or the demolition and bulldozing of poor people's homes. I had firsthand knowledge of their actions.

When I first started the ministry, a little nine-year-old girl, Natasha, became attached to me. I unofficially took responsibility for her and sent her to school, and she stayed around me until she became an adult, even to this day at 26 years old. Now, her own daughter wants to be a doctor. The education available for the poor in rural Jamaica is usually substandard, and if a child is to have a chance at a good education, he or she must gain a place in one of the traditional high schools. Perhaps Natasha's child will have a chance if she is sent to a boarding school.

Natasha lived in a little one-room shack that she had built herself, attaching it onto her mother's one-room shack which was built on government land. One day they were ordered off the land and given 24 hours' notice to evacuate by the UDC before a bulldozer would come and tear it down. This was a common occurrence all over the island. Natasha called me in the United States to inform me and to ask what she should do. There was nothing I could do to help, being so far away in Indiana. I felt completely helpless and frustrated at not being able to help her.

Natasha was small and pretty with a smile that would light up a room. Her father had been murdered as he sat one evening tending a fire. There seemed to be no future for her or her family. They existed from day to day, trying to eke out enough food to feed Natasha and her two sisters and Natasha's daughter.

But being the smart girl that she was, she decided to take matters into her own hands. Instead of allowing the UDC to bulldoze her house, she tore the house down herself, walked it up the mountain, board by board, to a spot that a wealthy man gave the family, and rebuilt the room herself. When I got back to the island, our ministry, along with another team member, built her a nice house. The land given them was twenty feet by fifty feet, and we were able to build three houses on the plot. Her mother, older sister, and Natasha now live on land that will not be taken away by the government.

The village men anxiously reported what the UDC man had told them. "Miss Kit, him say that we have to get the blocks off the land by tomorrow as this is government land and we all going be in serious trouble."

I thought for a second, and then told the men, "DON'T YOU DARE TOUCH ONE BLOCK! We have prayed and believed for that land and that is that." They looked at me as if I had lost my mind, but I told them, "Our God is bigger than the Jamaican government." They all walked away scratching their heads in disbelief. I know they thought I had lost my mind.

CHAPTER EIGHTEEN
MIRACLE ON THE MOUNTAIN

The blocks remained on the lot, and the UDC man never came back until a year later when the prime minister of Jamaica, P.J. Patterson, came to the mountain. The mountain was part of the prime minister's constituency, and he came with his entourage, his bodyguards, his band, a tent, and food for everyone on the mountain. After all, there were at least 350 votes in the village, and he was seeking reelection in a few months' time.

The day of the big function, I put on my best dress and a large hat and went to the tent when the ceremony was about to begin. After all the official speeches and guests were introduced, I raised my hand during the period set aside for interested parties to ask questions. I had decided to ask about the land. The MC asked me to come up to the mike so everyone could hear me. I introduced myself and my mission, Jesus for Jamaica, but don't remember what all I said after that because I was really scared out of my wits.

I recognized the UDC man as part of the prime minister's official party, along with policemen and other local and national politicians. But whatever I said must have made sense because afterward, the prime minister came up to me, gently taking me by my elbow.

Prime Minister Patterson is a tall, elegant man with old-world manners and a courtly charm. He walked me a little way from the crowd and noise. "Miss Kit, can we have a word? The land you want, is it somewhere that we can drive to?"

I snapped out of my daze immediately and said, "Sir, we can walk to the land," and I set off, holding firmly to his hand, dragging him along with me.

So there we were, the prime minister of Jamaica, his bodyguards, and his entire entourage of political supporters and hangers-on, walking with me, dodging donkey poo as we walked to where the 600 cement blocks were still sitting. Grass was growing up between the blocks, and as we stood and gazed at the site, he turned to the head of UDC and told him, "Have the surveyors come next week and give her all the land she wants." I couldn't believe my ears.

A miracle had taken place right there on that mountainside. We had prayed, believed, and kept faith that the land would be ours someday, and although the Jamaican government never gives land away, God had softened their hearts, and our faith in God had brought in the harvest. The clinic has been a work in progress, with many man hours and tons of donated money to get it where it is today. The clinic was named the Daynee-Anne Ball Memorial Clinic in honor of Daynee-Anne.

CHAPTER NINETEEN

HARD TIMES, HARD CHOICES

Life in the village was getting worse. Fishermen were disappearing at sea, and the fishing was down for reasons nobody could explain. Therefore, there was no money to buy the fruit and vegetables in the market. Everyone was suffering, but more so the children. The poor of the rural villages surrounding our mission base have no chance in life; there are no jobs in this area, no prospect of a job, no welfare or food banks, no clothing bank, not even a family member with enough money to get a loan from. Many eat only flour dumplings or perhaps some oats or cornmeal porridge for the whole day. Most households were five to ten people living in a small one-room house, cooking on open fires outside, no running water, no sanitary plumbing, and most times, there was no electricity. They used oil lanterns, and many times I was told, they went to bed hungry. Sometimes they use black plastic bags to go to the toilet in…these are called scandal bags.

But the heartening thing about these people is that they never feel sorry for themselves, a trait that I wish I could have. One of my helpers, Diana, called me one day as I was with my family on the North Coast. My daughter and my three granddaughters were with me for a week's visit. Diana had just received a call telling her that her house was on fire. By the time we got back to Whitehouse, her house was nothing but ashes. Her brother had set the house on fire because he was upset with her. She lost everything. The only thing left was the clothes on her four children's backs and the clothes she was wearing. The children moved into three different relatives' homes, and Diana moved in with me. By then, my cottage was finished and I had room for her.

When the next mission team arrived, we were able to build another house for her and furnish it. We also replaced her clothing and clothing for the children, as well as most household items. She was delighted and forever grateful and is still one of my faithful helpers. During the week she now stays in a small guesthouse that I recently built on my property. She goes home on weekends, but during the week she cleans and cooks for me and looks after my two dogs whenever I go home to the States. She is more than a helper; she is my friend.

PART FOUR

CHAPTER ONE

LIFE IN PARADISE

The day started out like any other day in "paradise." The bright sun-rays were glistening on the shimmering blue waters of the cove that sheltered my beach cottage. The cottage was a two-story wooden house built on concrete pillars and set back from the roadway. The wraparound porch afforded a spectacular view of the bay and was high enough to allow me the luxury of being able to sleep at nights with the windows and doors open to catch the cooling cross breeze blowing off the sea and the mountains. But before the end of the day, all that would change.

As I walked through the yard with the morning's first cup of cof-fee, my gaze fell on the cactuses that Ninja had planted before the rainy season started. They were now well rooted and thriving, and the rest of the garden was beginning to take shape. The Doctor Birds were buzzing around the hibiscus blooms, and the morning air was crisp, clean, and still full of the scent of the night blooming jasmine that grew wild on the barbed wire fence that separated my property from the neighboring lot.

The sight of the plants, while bringing a smile to my face, also brought a worried frown as well. The frown appeared when I recalled my talk with Ninja the previous evening. I had a B-I-G problem. Ninja was madly in love with me; obsessively, crazily, dangerously in love with me.

It was just before sunset, when I had wandered over to his little cottage in the back garden on a whim. Ninja had just finished painting the front of the steps in the red oxide that most Jamaicans used to stain their floor and steps. I watched him head over to the seaside to the dugout canoe he kept tied on the beach. From past experience, I knew that he was off to check his lobster pots for the evening.

I never intended to enter the room. I just wanted to look at the steps, but a glimpse of a picture of me on the wall in the house that faced the door made me step across the threshold to have a better look. It was more than I had bargained for. There were pictures of me, twenty in all, in the same pose, plastered all over the wooden walls. They were pictures I had brought to Jamaica after my last visit home, and were intended as gifts for friends. I didn't even know they were missing and couldn't imagine how he had managed to get hold of them, but there they were. My initial shock turned to fright as the implications began to dawn on me.

Yes, I trusted Ninja implicitly, but this was not just creepy; it was downright scary. I could not stop the scream of terror that escaped my lips when I turned around and saw Ninja standing in the doorway, his face wreathed in anger, tinged with shame.

"What you doing fassing in my things?" he demanded. While his voice was angry, I also detected that he was also equally as frightened as I was.

"What the hell is this?" I blurted. "Why do you have my pictures? How did you get them and ... Oh my God, what sort of a situation have I caused?" I wailed. Maybe it was the sight of me crying, or the shock of being discovered, but Ninja couldn't hold back anymore.

"I tek the picture them because is the only way I can have you," he shouted, while trying to keep his voice from cracking. "Everybody know dat I love you. Is only you one don't see it. Is only you one don't notice. I would do anything for you."

I was floored by the confession. Ninja had a talent for being the project manager and had learned quickly and was always eager to help, and I knew he would lay his life down for me, for which I was grateful since not many people in the span of a lifetime will have someone that is so very loyal. I felt he truly had a servant's heart and was devoted. He was bodyguard, a fabulous cook, and wouldn't let me pick up a broom or a rake. He maintained the yard and planted the garden and even cleaned the house. But I couldn't imagine myself taking Ninja as a lover. He was 30 years my junior, for God's sake.

As I recovered my composure, I tried to let him down easy. "Ninja, you know I am a married woman. I can't encourage you to love me. Plus, I am too old for you. You need to bury your feelings and find a nice young girl to marry."

But Ninja wasn't ready to give up and just kept shaking his head. "I can't un-love you, Kit. I love you already," he said sadly. "I live to have you as my queen." The last came out as a wail as he couldn't hold back the tears anymore, and broke down crying like a baby. Instinctively, I reached to hug him, but the immediate look of glee on his face was the last straw for me. I immediately pulled back and pushed him away.

"If you can't bury those feelings, then I won't allow you to come around me," I threatened angrily, as I fled back to my house. But we both knew that it was an empty threat, since I had come to rely on him and be dependent on him. That night, I spent a restless night tossing and turning in my bamboo bed, waking from time to time from dreams I could not remember. My bamboo bed with it's white flowing mosquito netting and tropical bed spread has been my refuge. It was always a place I could go and forget all the worries of the day. But this night was different. Maybe it was what was to happen in the coming days but the sleep would not come. Something was troubling my spirit. I got up out of bed and headed for the garden.

It was these thoughts that occupied my mind as I wandered the garden and admired the beauty of nature. I had made up my mind. I would have to find the courage to send Ninja away. There was nothing else to be done. It was not a healthy relationship. And if they haven't started already, people were sure to start talking soon.

It was with great hurt in my heart that I headed to the backyard to find Ninja and tell him of my decision.

That was when I had a "visit" from the "big man" and my days in paradise would never be the same again.

CHAPTER TWO

TROUBLE IN PARADISE

I had just started down the pathway toward the back gate when the big black truck pulled into my driveway. My mind, from years of being a traffic cop, automatically registered the details: latest model, custom-designed Ford F150, with oversized tires and shiny chrome rims that cost more than what I spent in a year for groceries. The windows, including the windshield, were tinted black with reflective tint, so it was impossible to see inside the vehicle. But as the vehicle pulled up next to me, the driver-side window smoothly slid down.

A cloud of smoke laced with the pungent smell of the local "sensimilla" ganja wafted through the window, punctuated by the heavy bass and drum of the current dancehall "riddim" that was blasting on the truck's stereo system.

My first thought was that some teenage Kingston "tourists" had made a wrong turn and were seeking directions. But as the cloud of ganja smoke cleared and a clearer image emerged, I found myself facing a malevolent glare from a vaguely familiar face. I recoiled visibly when I realized that I was looking at the man I had heard Jamaicans in the village refer to as "the big man."

The big man was reputed to be the biggest drug smuggler, the one don, the head boss man, the capo di tutti capi, the godfather if you want to call him that. I had seen him from a distance on several occasions. He could usually be seen in the village square conducting "business" in the bar, doling out his fear or favors, depending on the circumstances. He was usually surrounded by his posse of three or four young toughs the people called "shottas."

"What you 'fraid of, white girl?" he drawled while puffing on his ganja "spliff" the size of a Cohiba cigar and continuing to glare at me. "Why yuh so jumpy? Ah just checking yuh like a good neighbor should." His glare was now replaced by a leering grin that made me think of Little Red Riding Hood's big bad wolf.

If this approach was intended to put me at ease, it was not working. He did not look at me like a friendly neighbor. His look was not a pleasant look. In fact, the look turned my blood cold and shook my life pretty badly. But I had faced bullies all my life, and this one was no different. Never let them see you sweat.

"This is private property. How may I help you?" I asked in my best Midwest twang, mustering up as much bravado as I could, given that I was quaking in my boots.

"Private property??" bellowed Mr. Big, blowing a cloud of smoke in my face. "A hope yuh understand say the whole of this place is private property. Not just your yard. Everybody yard is private property. Even the seaside is private property. So see and blind and hear and deaf. You better not be checking anything. You think I don't know who you is, but I see and know everything. Remember that. I have eyes all in the back of my head." And with that parting salvo, the window slid back up, and the truck rolled out of the driveway and sped up the road to the sound of squealing tires and the smell of burning rubber.

I was shaking badly as I watched the truck reverse down the driveway. It took all my courage not to turn tail and run inside. But I forced myself to calmly open the back garden gate that allowed my entry to my house through the small room that served as living room, dining room, and kitchen. I had barely reached inside when the sound of more squealing tires registered on my consciousness.

At first I thought it was the "big man" in the black truck coming back, so I quickly walked to the kitchen window which overlooks the driveway and the road to get a better look outside. But I realized that the squeals were coming from the opposite direction from where "Mr. Big's" truck had been headed. And before I had time to clearly take in all the details, a powerful motorbike with a fully helmeted and visored rider dressed in black leather from head to toe and a similarly attired pillion rider high on the back, roared around the corner. As they drew alongside my yard, the pillion rider raised his arm and two shots rang out.

CHAPTER THREE

MR. BIG

With reflexes still sharp from my years of police training, I had just enough time to throw my body under the wooden dining table as the bullets whizzed through the open kitchen window and lodged in the concrete wall opposite where I had been standing.

As I lay curled under the table shivering, Ninja came pounding through the door, a look of complete horror etched on his face. "Kit, Kit!! You all right? You get shot? Lord God, ah wah dis, Lord?" he wailed. He had been inside his garden cottage and did not yet know of my visit from Mr. Big.

"I'm okay. Help me to get up from under this table," I gasped, holding out my shaking hand for assistance. Ninja helped me up, then got me a glass of water from the fridge. I assured him that I had not been hit by the bullets.

As I tried to steady my visibly shaking hands enough to drink some of the water Ninja had handed me, I quickly filled him in on Mr. Big's visit, our talk, and the implied threat. And as I recounted the incident, the full horror of the situation began to come home to me. "What in the world am I doing here?" I bawled. "I must be out of my mind. What did he mean that he knew who I am?"

Ninja, who was still trying to get a grip on his own emotions, couldn't find the words to provide an answer, so he just stared at me.

But I really didn't expect an answer. My questions were directed at myself and the Lord. As I paced the floor around the wooden table that had recently served as my shield and protector I gave a silent prayer thanking God for earthquake and bomb drills in elementary schools in America. But my questions didn't stop: "Have I worked so hard in this life to lose it all with this crazy and unpredictable situation? Have I painted myself into a corner?" I didn't have the answers yet, but I knew they would come.

By now, Ninja had recovered from his shock enough to grasp some of what I was saying. "You think Mr. Big think you know something?" he asked. "But you don't know anything? Do you? What you going to do?"

I'm sure I gave him a look that he had never seen before. I had always looked at him with kindness before. There was nothing kind in this look or the tone of my answer as I started pacing again, holding my head between my hands and massaging my temples furiously. "Ninja, I don't know anything! I don't know where this is coming from," I shouted, still trying to get my body and emotions under control. "I don't know what to do. What will I do? What will I do?" But I knew that panicking and crying was not going to give me the answers. I knew that I needed to calm down if I was going to be able to process everything. "I feel as if my head is about to explode, Ninja. I feel as if my brain is being squeezed."

I was focusing on the fear too much and not functioning as I should. I had dealt with this before. The death threats, the gunshots, the terror. *But that was then—back there—that other life.* I didn't expect it here. I needed to clear my brain before I could make sense of everything. Finally, I took a deep breath and put my best smile on. It didn't fool Ninja, but he didn't comment. "Okay, Ninja," I started, "I need to get back to normal now. We have things to do. I need to put this aside for a while." And with that, I headed up the spiral stairs to my living quarters.

CHAPTER FOUR

JAMAICAN NINJA

Ninja watched as I climbed the stairs and made sure I had reached to the top before he turned and headed back to his garden cottage. He too needed to think, to sort through the jumbled thoughts tumbling through his brain. *Why did "the big man" come to see Kit? What does "Mr. Big" know? What did he think that she knew? And what is this "good neighbor" business?*

The confrontation with me the evening before had rattled him and put Ninja on his guard. It was a very close call that could have played out differently. Leaving the cottage door open was a bad mistake, but he had managed to diffuse the situation when I saw the pictures, and it had ended much better than he had expected. I did not go off as badly as I could have. Yes, I was mad as hell. But he could deal with that.

He had faced my wrath before, and he had overcome. He could deal with me. The fact that he was now my trusted confidant and bodyguard was proof positive.

As he thought of his bodyguard role, Ninja couldn't help but chuckle to himself as he flashed on the lyrics of a popular reggae song that asked "*. . . but who is guarding the bodyguard?*"

As a man of thirty-five, Ninja had known Kit for more than half his life. He could remember the first time he met her, as if it were yesterday, never mind that he was only fifteen years old at the time. She had come to his village leading a group of missionaries who had set up a giant tent on a large open lot and built a bamboo church.

The group members were all white foreigners who seemed to be as befuddled by their surroundings as the villagers were by them. During the day, some of the group's members who were doctors and nurses conducted a medical clinic to give free checkups to the people and take their blood pressure and check their sugar level. At night, they would conduct their religious crusade in the bamboo church to bless and minister to those who were interested.

Ninja had been living on the side of a mountain with his extended family in a home that was falling down around him. Although he had family on the mountain, they really paid no attention to him. There were times he seemed all alone. All alone, living in a two-room shack with five other people.

Ninja's extended family consisted of his grandmother, who was his mother's mother, his father sometimes, his brother Lew who was just turning ten and worshipped Ninja, and his sister Sandra who was only two years older than him, but looked and acted much older. She saw Ninja as a pest and wanted nothing to do with him that did not involve insults and sometimes physical pain. She had a wicked left hook when she was "provoked," and it seemed that everything that he did "provoked" her.

CHAPTER FIVE

FEAR

I traveled with fear everywhere I went that day. As I walked in the market, when I visited the base camp, even at the church meeting I attended in the afternoon. The events of the morning had made a lasting impression on me, and I knew it was time to do what I had hoped I wouldn't have to. But it was clear: I needed to follow up on the application I had put in for a firearm permit four months earlier.

One evening a few months earlier, a "go-fast" boat came into the bay and a Hispanic-looking man, with the help of Jamaicans, unloaded several large bales and drums. I had also noticed the man for most of the week, walking up and down the beach and occasionally talking on a cell phone. Boats came in a few more times during the week, and I had a bird's-eye view of the happenings in the bay where I held children's Bible class each Saturday.

The children who came to Saturday Bible class were all from very poor backgrounds and it was usual for me to take them to the beach and feed them lunch, as many had walked miles to attend the class. The Saturday after I first saw the man in the bay as I walked the children to the beach, which was only a mere 100 feet from the big tree I had the Bible class under, the man was there, as usual, talking on a cell phone. He said something in broken English, and it was then that I realized that he was not a Jamaican. I hurried the more than twenty children off the beach and went back to the base camp.

When I returned home from the base camp, I found Ninja in the yard and told him about the man on the beach. That was when I learned that the boat had come from Colombia with a large load of cocaine.

"He is a Colombian," Ninja said. "Him waiting for information about when another boat going to arrive."

"Are you sure of that, Ninja?" I was shocked at his casual tone.

"Yeah, man. The big man dem send Colombians here to make sure that their stuff reach safe and put them at different spots on the beach in the places where they landing the boats, and then call them men to give the word when the boat will come to their location. They don't let them know in advance about where the load will arrive because the Jamaican government and the Americans join together as 'Kingfish Operations' and have helicopters and fast boats to shoot the Colombians out of the water."

Ninja's matter-of-fact explanation left me flabbergasted, but I made no comment as he continued speaking. "When the Kingfish shoot them up, them have to throw the cocaine out into the sea and them lose a lot of money, but our fisherman dem that find the stuff become rich overnight. You can always tell when a fisherman find the 'stuff' because him build big house right away."

CHAPTER SIX

DANGER

I always recognized that life in Jamaica was rough and at times could be very dangerous. It was not unusual now to have shootouts in the village, and I had been awakened many times by gunshots in the village. But I always prayed when I would hear the shots. Throughout my time in Jamaica, I had always felt that no one would harm me as most knew that they would be dead meat if they did anything to me or the teams of people I brought to Jamaica to help with the mission.

My police days, or glory days, as some of the cops described it, were over, but I often thought that God had given me boldness and courage to prepare me for the work ahead in Jamaica. I truly believed that my police days were a training ground for my later years and had served to give me what I liked to think of as "holy boldness." I felt that I could go anywhere, do anything as I always had God at my side, but now, I tried very hard not to go out after dark as I realized that the days of peace were over.

In the villages I quickly learned that the law was in the hands of the people and vigilante justice was the norm. If someone stole or broke into their little houses, the village men would run down the suspect and beat him to death. It was one such occurrence, coupled with the Colombians on the beach, that made me decide to apply for a gun permit. After all, I had always carried a gun in the States, and, sad to say, I really felt I needed a gun here in paradise.

Recently, a man, high from smoking crack cocaine, had chopped off his girlfriend's head with a machete. Two villages, one in which the ministry had its outreach and another close by, gathered their men together, chased the suspect by car and on foot, and he ended up being cornered at the entrance of the base camp. They beheaded him, then cut his arms and privates off, throwing them all over the road. Later when the hearse came to pick up what was left of the body, the villagers blocked the road, opened the hearse, and pulled out the body and further mutilated it by cutting off his legs.

I had made the trip the next day to Savannah La Mar, or Sav, as the locals referred to the capital town of the parish of Westmoreland where all local and official government offices were located, and had visited the police department. The police station was nothing like the station I was used to in Muncie. It was small and crowded with people making complaints, relatives trying to see persons detained by the police, and lawyers trying to arrange bail for clients. There was a din of noise that came from the area that I assumed was the holding area for prisoners, from the dirty walls and the stench that emanated from it when the wind blew through the small barred window.

The front information counter was manned by a female special constable, or what Ninja called, "blue seam" for the blue stripe that ran down the sides of the uniform skirt she wore and the blue band that wrapped around the brim of the hat that sat on top of her hair which was styled in fat, tightly rolled curls that reminded Kit of link sausages.

Ninja had once explained to me that blue seams were really like deputy police who assisted the "real police, or red seam." They did not carry guns and did not have much power. The female constables were usually used to do clerical work in the police stations, while the men were usually put on foot patrols in the market and on the main street to regulate the many vendors who hawked their wares to pedestrians. They were also expected to keep order among the minibuses and taxis that crowded the capital streets, jockeying and racing to get passengers.

The female special constable had a large ledger that covered almost the whole top of the battered, blue and white Formica counter she sat behind. The ledger was used to record the statements of persons making official complaints. The constable took her time, writing the statements in a neat handwriting with rounded, well formed letters. She consulted a small dictionary from time to time to check the correct spelling of some words. This meant that each statement took a long time to record.

I had stood in line in the hot office for over two hours, when a police officer dressed in the brown khaki uniform of a superintendent, medals and badges gleaming on his pocket, came through the door behind the counter where the "blue seam" sat. On seeing a white woman in line, a rare and unusual occurrence since the police station was usually populated by Jamaicans, he came over and asked what I needed. When I had told him that I wanted to apply for a gun permit, he burst out laughing as if he had just been told a very funny joke. Everybody in the room turned to stare at us.

"Madame, do you know what you are asking?" he inquired, the amused look still on his face, as he took my elbow and guided me out of the crowded room, past the battered counter, and through the door behind the female constable. "That is not an everyday request you have there," he concluded as he ushered me to a chair in the back room we had entered.

As I looked around the small, cluttered office, I couldn't help but smile. "What are you smiling about, ma'am?" the superintendent asked.

And before I thought about it, I gave him an honest response. "It reminds me of my old office when I was a police investigator in America," I responded. And so it did.

CHAPTER SEVEN

ENTERTAINING THE SUPERINTENDENT

The chair on which the superintendent had seated Kit was a gray metal frame, with a seat upholstered in black simulated leather that had seen many backsides and much better days. It faced a wooden desk that was the same as the one Kit had in her old office, except this one was a good twenty years older and had more battle scars than her old one did. The swivel armchair that sat behind the desk, and in which the superintendent had squeezed his large frame, was a little more modern and had a beaded back-massaging mat covering the upholstered back and seat. A battered four-drawer filing cabinet and a small bookshelf overflowing with files and law books completed the office furnishings.

"Okay, let's start over," the superintendent said, folding his hands, palms down on the desk. "Let me introduce myself. I am Senior Superintendent Glen Burton. And, let me get this straight. You used to be a police investigator in America, and you want to apply for a gun permit. Do I have it right?" he inquired, looking at me with a smile that did not reach his eyes. Being an old hand at questioning suspects, I recognized the technique immediately. Put the suspect at ease before putting on the pressure.

"Yes, on both counts," I responded in my best twang, with a smile on my face. I too could play the game. And as my mama used to say, "You catch more flies with honey than vinegar."

"Will you be able to help me with the gun permit, Superintendent Burton?" I asked innocently. But the superintendent wasn't that easy. He was just getting started.

"We'll get to that later," he said, waving his hand impatiently. "First of all, who are you? What's your name, and why on earth would a nice white lady like you need a gun?"

When I had set out to get a gun permit, I didn't expect to have a problem. After all, there seemed to be a lot of guns in Jamaica, so how difficult could it be to get a permit? I assumed that like in Indiana, all you had to do was fill out an application for a gun permit, pay the requisite fee, and wait the five days it takes for the permit to arrive in the mail. Okay. This being Jamaica, and from past experience with the slow pace of the wheels of Jamaican government agencies, I figured it would take about a month, give or take a few days.

But, as I looked at the superintendent's face, I realized I was totally wrong. This was not going to be as easy as I had hoped. But, never one to back down from a challenge, I decided to plow right in. "I am Kit Belknap," I replied, holding out my right hand for a handshake. "Pleased to meet you, Superintendent Burton," I gushed, pumping his large hand firmly. "Please forgive my rudeness. I should have intro-duced myself before when you rescued me from that line outside," I said, apologizing. "Oh, and never mind about me being an investigator in America. That was a long time ago. I am a missionary now," I said, attempting to brush aside the question.

Superintendent Burton was not letting it go. "You are a missionary who used to be a police investigator, and now you want a gun? This gets better and better, lady."

He reached for a bunch of keys that had been lying on the desk, se-lected the smallest one on the bunch, and opened the bottom drawer of the desk, from which he pulled out a file folder with a sheaf of forms.

"This is the paperwork to apply for a firearm license that you are required to complete," he explained, pulling a set of the forms from the file folder and setting it in the middle of the desktop. "But before we get started on the forms, tell me some more about your missionary work in Jamaica."

CHAPTER EIGHT

RECOUNTING THE MINISTRY

Irealized that he was serious, and therefore made the decision to spend some time with him. "I think we better get comfortable, because this is going to take a while," I warned as I settled back into my chair. Somehow, this gentleman made me feel at ease, and maybe I needed to unburden my soul to a stranger, but whatever the reason, I decided to trust the sup.

Superintendent Burton made no comment, only indicating that I should continue. If he had time to listen while I recount every year of my life, I would.

"I was not sure at first why I had such a burden for the people," I continued, "but as time went by, I was sure it had been a direct call on my life. Things just started to make sense on why I ended up in a foreign country. I am here, called by God. Of that, I am very sure. I am His instrument, and God just happened to pick Jamaica for me."

Superintendent Burton shifted lower on his beaded backrest and settled back with his arms folded across his ample chest. I was not sure if he was amused or bemused, but it was clear that no forms would be filled out until he had heard my story. So I too settled my backside into the chair seat, leaned back, and continued with my story.

"The first time my husband and I came here on a cruise twenty years ago, I knew nothing about this place called Jamaica, not even knowing where it was located on the map. I thought it was located somewhere near Puerto Rico. Sure, I had heard the name back in

Indiana, and some of my colleagues had even been here on short trips, but I never knew it was such a country of contrasts." Jamaica had come up in investigations of drug trade; that is about all I knew.

While I was glad to be able to speak with a fellow law-enforcement professional, I still wasn't sure how much I could trust Senior Superintendent Glen Burton, so I didn't feel the need to elaborate on which colleagues and how they came to visit or how brief the visit was. "I can't believe that sixteen years of ministry and outreach has gone by in the wink of an eye. Here I am, in a country that I did not choose, living in a village I did not choose, and with people I do not always understand. It has been a day-to-day learning experience, sometimes scary, many times rewarding, and sometimes downright funny. Boy, do I have some funny stories. Want to hear one, Superintendent Burton?"

Superintendent Burton wasn't sure what the strange white lady would consider a "funny story," but he had no intention of going anywhere else until he had heard everything I had to say, and then some. So he nodded eagerly, hoping I wouldn't decide to clam up.

"After I started our mission, I went back to Indiana and in eighteen months raised enough money and recruited thirty-seven people to join in the effort of building a church on land on the mountainside. With bake sales, rummage sales, donations from churches and merchants, we were able to make the trip back to the island. In those days, there were no phones, very few cars, and communication was hard to establish in Jamaica.

"The majority of the team stayed in a villa and on the nearby beach in cramped quarters while two of the men stayed in a tent close to the worksite. Jamaica had been experiencing a severe drought with no rain or ways to find water for over three months. White marl was brought in to make the church floor, and we had to have water to set the marl which we knew would turn into a cement-type foundation. We began praying for rain every day and night.

"One evening as the outreach team returned to our quarters in the villa, we were given a message from the worksite. Word had been passed down that the two white men on the mountain had lost their minds and were running up and down the trail, shouting, flinging their hands in the air, and jumping up and down.

"At first, we were all very concerned, but that changed when we found out the next day that rain had started to fall, and it was just enough to set the marl. The two guys were running up and down the village praising God for the miracle. The villagers had never seen anything like this, so they thought the men had gone mad."

Superintendent Burton wasn't sure what part of the story she considered funny, or even if she meant that the story was "hah-hah" funny or "strange" funny. White women were a strange breed, and this one was sounding stranger than the usual ones he met in this part of town. But he smiled politely, while nodding to encourage me to continue. Somehow he was sure that they were not anywhere near the real reason for her visit.

As I started to speak again, the superintendent eased out of his chair, holding his hand out to make me pause in my narrative. "Just a minute, madam. Take a break and let me get us some refreshments. Would a Ting or Ginger Beer be okay?"

I was a little surprised that he was offering refreshments. From what I knew, the Jamaican police was not in the habit of entertaining. But then again, I wasn't a Jamaican criminal or suspect. And, maybe, just maybe, he was genuinely interested in my story. "A Ting will be fine, Sup, and a glass of ice water as well, if possible," I smiled and replied politely.

The sup squeezed his bulky frame from behind the desk and stuck his head out the door and asked the "blue seam" to get two Tings and two glasses of iced water. Then he returned to his seat and sat observing this strange white woman sitting in front of him.

Senior Superintendent Glen Burton, officer in charge of Operation Kingfish for all of the Jamaican south coast, was just as surprised that he was offering refreshments, but his instincts told him that they would need a lot more liquid before he was finished with her story. And, yes, he was genuinely interested in what she was saying. In fact, he did not want to miss a word of what she was saying. When the "blue seam" came in, balancing a tray with the Tings and iced waters, the sup cleared a space on his desk, and she placed the cold drinks before them.

I took a sip of my iced water, leaving the Ting for after I had finished the water. I wanted to pour the Ting over the ice to dilute it a little. I found the sweet grapefruit taste of the drink a little too strong and preferred to tame it with ice. After my first sip of water, I made to start talking again, but the sup was still drinking his Ting, straight from the bottle, and waved me to wait. After he had drained the bottle dry and exhaled a satisfied sigh, he raised his glass of iced water and guzzled half the contents and again sat back with a satisfied sigh, this time with a grin before waving me to continue.

"Go on now, madam. I am listening."

I wasn't sure that Superintendent Burton was aware of or prepared for the flood of memories he had unearthed. But now that I had started, I couldn't stop, and so I continued telling him about my ministry and life in Jamaica. And anyways, he had asked.

Now it seemed his turn to tell me some of his life stories.

CHAPTER NINE

SUPERINTENDENT'S STORY

Superintendent Burton sat patiently and spent another two hours listening about the mission and its accomplishments. As a Christian man serving in the Jamaican police force, life had not been easy for the superintendent. He began telling me about his life and career. He had been a green recruit at the police academy when he had heard God's call and had a notion that he should not only heed the Word of God, but become a living testimony and vessel for the Holy Word. Having recognized that, then "Squaddie" Burton had made the decision to be an honest, upright, and fair policeman. This made him the exception rather than the rule among his fellow recruits. The norm was for policemen to be little more than legal criminals hiding behind the protection of the state, politicians, and a uniform and gun.

He told me he was from Whithorn, a village in the hills of Westmoreland. The majority of his classmates from the police training academy came from tough inner-city communities like Tivoli Gardens, Trench Town, Denham Town, and rural ghettos of Spanish Town, Montego Bay, and May Pen. During his time at the academy, he often wondered why so many of the rank-and-file policemen came from these areas. It was explained to him by an officer who had seen the promise in him, taken him under his wing, and invited him to join the Christian Officers Association, a grouping of security officers in the police, military, and correctional services.

"This usually means that those recommended by the members of Parliament are the youths they or their area leaders have recruited early on as boys, and the area leaders have supported and encouraged through school, with a view to having their talents and abilities available to them later on." He went on to inform Glen that some inner-city communities even had their own paramilitary force that maintained order in the community and dispensed their own brand of justice as judge, jury, and executioner. Boys were trained from an early age to shoot, rob, steal, and deal drugs. As the superintendent continued to tell me about his life, a new respect was formed in my mind.

"The boys who are targeted for special attention are usually from single-parent homes with fathers being largely missing in action and the area leader or 'don' being the only father figure available to them. The flashy lifestyle of the don and his ability to provide money and material goods to the mothers and girls of the community ensures the don's primacy and the loyalty of these women who often turn a blind eye to their men and sons' transgressions, while having to give their daughters to the dons and their minions."

Glen said he was shocked at this revelation. Coming from rural Jamaica, he was completely unaware of how things were in the urban ghettos of the bigger towns, but listened intently to what his friend had to say.

"When the security forces advertise for recruits, the dons and politicians in certain communities quickly snap up the opportunity to place their favored ones on the inside. This comes in very handy for the dons and politicians since having these men in their pockets often proves to be a valuable asset, especially when they get caught in nefarious actions and need to have evidence 'disappear' or falsified, or even witnesses threatened or whatever is necessary to ensure their cooperation."

Superintendent Glen Burton had worked closely with the prime minister as bodyguard for several years until his promotion to superintendent, and when the Americans had joined with the Jamaican Constabulary Force to start Operation Kingfish to interdict and arrest the flow of drugs in and out of the island, he had been given the opportunity to take university courses in law enforcement in the U.S. at the FBI Academy in Washington. When he returned home he was promoted to senior superintendent and was put in charge of all of Kingfish operations in the southwest of Jamaica, which included Westmoreland and St. Elizabeth.

He had been working tirelessly at his task, but the vast expanse of coastline and coves along the Westmoreland and St. Elizabeth shores oftentimes proved to be virtually impossible to patrol and protect. He knew that there were policemen on his squad that were involved with protecting the drugs coming in by boat from Colombia, and he was determined to find them and rout them out. He just needed to catch a break, and when I had started talking to him, he knew that his prayers had been answered. God had sent him the break he needed.

"Look," he said, "you need a gun permit, we need a vantage point to observe boats in and out of the bay. I'll send one of my men to stay on your property, that is, if you can house one."

"Oh, sure," I replied. "I have a tree house that sleeps three, has it's own plumbing, and if he doesn't mind 'un-fancy,' then I'm sure it would work. It's a little primitive and Jamaican style, but it is comfortable."

"Okay, let me call one of my Kingfish officers, and he will accompany you home."

A few minutes later, a man approximately forty years old walked in the room. Superintendent Burton introduced him as one of his finest and most trusted officers. I was still not sure all of this was worth a gun permit, but if I could help in any way to curtail the drug traffic, then I was all for it.

The ride back to Whitehouse with the bodyguard/Kingfish officer was a little strained. The officer was very quiet and seemed to be miles away in thought. He was thirty-four years old he told me and had a serious girlfriend with two babies. I failed to tell him any of my background as I figured that could wait until I got to know him a little better.

I had my helper change the sheets in the tree house and take ice water for the bedside. When Ninja realized what was going on, he turned to me and said, "Guess you don't need me here anymore."

I was in no mood to try to explain anything, and he turned and went out the gate, slamming it behind him.

The following days were uneventful. The days were warm with the typical tropical breezes and the sound of the sea hitting the beach. It was quiet and just peaceful and lovely. My new bodyguard, Mitch, kept busy with his binoculars and constant cell phone calls. I noticed that he stayed out of sight of anyone who might pass on the beach. The foliage around my cottage was a thick jungle, just the way I liked it. Ninja and I had planted most of the trees and plants, forgetting that they would soon be huge and overtaking each other. It made for a very tropical and jungle-looking area. Narrow paths wandered in and out of the foliage. A small pond with brightly colored fish and a fountain completed the area.

Mitch seemed to enjoy the privacy that the garden provided, and at times, I was not sure he was around. He only came to the main house to fix himself some coffee or a quick snack. He was so humble and quiet, a true gentleman, and that made me feel he would rather not get to know me. Our conversations were few but always timely and always about the case. The conversations were informative and each time we talked, we discussed the possible actions we might take in case there were ever a boatload of drugs that would enter the bay.

He seemed very protective of me. He wanted me to understand the complexity of the problem. Other than that, he kept his distance from the main house.

Early one morning I heard voices coming from the beach. I alerted Mitch, and he crawled through the front garden and took up a position where he could see. I could watch out my kitchen window and noticed two pickup trucks arrive. To my surprise and horror, I realized that one of the trucks belonged to the big man. Seems as if the men were having a meeting of sorts. An hour later they left, leaving the beach empty and quiet again.

Mitch came into the kitchen where I was standing and told me that I was never to look out the window again and that Superintendent Burton was on his way to my house. Evening fell and a moon glowed against the sky full of twinkling stars. Sometimes evenings in Jamaica are magical with the soft moonlight and the smell and sound of the sea and night jasmine. Tonight seemed like one of those nights.

I retreated to my room, a little curious as to what might have been going on in the bay but also knowing this was not child's play. I needed to let the big boys play this game. From the veranda that my bed faced I could see quite a bit. Jamaican moonlight was shining bright that evening, and I was able to see when Sup. Burton arrived with a young man and they walked to the tree house.

In the far distance I heard the purr of a boat engine. As it got near, I could make out that it was a "go-fast" boat. They have a special sound about them, one that I have heard many times coming into the bay. I had seen a few boats unload their goods but had never told anyone. In Jamaica, you see nothing and you hear nothing. I stood in the shadows of my moonlit room and watched.

The two trucks that had been there earlier arrived. Five men got out of the two trucks, and then a black van pulled into the beach area. The boat arrived, the men helped hoist the boat to the sand, and onto the beach. This was a boat from Colombia, that was for sure. A mother lode of cocaine was surely on this boat. I felt my blood go cold. Then gunfire shattered the silent night. I jumped back away from the door.

I could see three figures run across my yard, toward the beach. *Oh no, they must realize that they are outnumbered. What should I do???* My police training told me I had to run to help them, but reality kicked in and said ... you don't even have a weapon! I heard yelling, then gunshots, at least four shots, and then the revving of motors. Next came the sound of tires hitting the asphalt, followed by silence. I ran down my stairs and out the gate to the beach. At this point, I had no fear.

Visions flashed across my brain as I ran. I saw my former police comrades almost as if they were running with me. I felt the pain of the mothers I had witnessed when they found out their children were on some type of drug. I saw the faces of my fellow officers who just found that they had been betrayed by the system. Each running step was a painful reminder of the years of fighting the drug cartel. I was totally out of breath by the time I reached the beach. I was not ready for the scene before me. Really, no one could ever be prepared for that.

I dropped down on my knees beside Mitch. He was facedown in the sand, dark blood staining the sand beside him. I rolled him over and brushed the sand from his face. He was attempting to say something. I placed my ear to his face "phone ... call" ... then he uttered, "Not worth. Go home ... forget ..." his voice trailing off to a mere whisper. "Not worth ..." then silence.

Superintendent Burton was laying faceup with his gun still in his hand. I located his cell phone and called for help.

It seemed like hours before I heard cars coming toward the beach. I held Mitch's limp body as I sat on the sand. I had realized the sup was not breathing. His call to duty was over; he had made his last call. I rocked Mitch back and forth in my lap, crying out to God to let this young man live. I sat in a pool of blood on the sand. The Jamaican moonlight made the scene seem more eerie, and now, the only sounds heard were the waves crashing against the beach and my sobbing.

Finally, cars, then trucks, arrived. I'm not even sure how many because by then I felt I had entered another world. A world that didn't matter; time standing still; a time when even your surroundings seem faded. I felt as if my purpose in life had come to a screeching halt.

As someone jerked Mitch out of my lap I could hear a scream. Then I realized the scream was coming from me. I turned and placed my face in the sand, trying to muffle the scream. A voice in my head began to reverberate. A scripture came to my mind ... Revelations 3:8. "I know thy works: behold, I have set before thee an open door, and no man can shut it." I lifted myself from the sand with tears falling from my eyes, and I began walking toward the cottage.

God hates injustice, and so do I.

CPSIA information can be obtained at www.ICGtesting.com
Printed in the USA
LVOW122321260413

331153LV00021B/1018/P